What if they knew?

What if they knew?

by Patricia Hermes

A Yearling Book

Published by
Dell Publishing Co., Inc.
1 Dag Hammarskjold Plaza
New York, New York 10017

Yearling ® TM 913705, Dell Publishing Co., Inc.

ISBN: 0-440-49515-6

Reprinted by arrangement with Harcourt Brace Jovanovich, Inc.

Printed in the United States of America
First Yearling printing—October 1981

CW

For those I love—Matthew,
and Paul and Mark and Tim and Matt,
and Jennifer,
and for "Grandfather"

1

I couldn't believe this was happening! How could they do this to me—my own parents? I read the letter again, and then again. I looked up at Grandma and Grandpa. They were sitting across the table from me, just looking at me. "I can't go to school here! I can't!" I said to them. "Mom and Daddy know that!"

"Honey. Now, honey," Grandma said. "All they're doing is something that's important to their future as well as yours. You know what your daddy said. It's important, necessary for his business, that he stay in London for a little while longer. It will only be until the end of the year."

I began to cry. "But they've been gone two whole months already—practically all summer!"

"I know, Jeremy," Grandma said. "But a few more months isn't going to matter that much, is it?"

"It's going to matter a lot," I said. "I told you—I can't go to school here!"

Grandma got up from the table. She went to the stove and came back with a pot and some dishes and started serving dinner. She acted just as she always did, as if there was nothing wrong at all.

"Jeremy," she said, putting a big helping of something on my plate, "when school starts next week, you're going to be surprised. Going to school in Brooklyn isn't going to be that different from going to school in Long Island. Now, why don't we just eat dinner? Everything's going to work out just fine."

I pushed away my plate and jumped up. I was really crying now. "I'm not eating dinner!" I said. "And I'm not staying here, either! You can't get me to!"

I ran into my bedroom and slammed the door. I dropped a pile of books on the floor. Then I opened a dresser drawer and slammed it shut again as hard as I could, about a thousand times.

I couldn't believe this! How could they *do* this to me?

I opened the bedroom door and slammed it shut again. The room shook. I didn't care. I slammed the door again, two more times, before Grandma came to my room.

"That's quite enough, Jeremy," she said quietly. She opened the door, pushing it back all the way. "Now leave it that way. Come sit down to dinner."

"I don't want dinner," I said.

"Well, sit down anyway," Grandma said. She stood at the door and waited till I went back to the kitchen.

I sat down at the table and stared at my plate.

"Jeremy," Grandma said, "Your mom and daddy are going to call tomorrow night to talk to you about it. Meanwhile, look at the bright side. You'll enjoy going to school here. You've made lots of friends this summer. The twins—Mimi and Libby—they're your age, aren't they? Maybe they'll be in the same class with you."

"They won't be in my class," I said, almost under my breath, "because I'm not going to school here."

Grandma sighed, but she didn't say anything more. She looked at Grandpa.

I looked at Grandpa, too. I really loved Grandpa. I was named after him, even though I'm a girl. He hadn't said anything since this all started, since Grandma first showed me the letter from my mom. He was just looking at me now, as if maybe he was waiting for me to say something.

"You understand, don't you?" I said to him. I couldn't tell what he was thinking, but I had to have *someone* on my side.

"I'm listening," he said quietly.

Grandma reached across the table. She poured a glass of milk from the pitcher and handed it to me. "Now, Jeremy," she said. "You're making too big a thing about all this."

"But you don't know what it's like!" I said to her. I was crying again. I couldn't help it. "You just don't know what it's like!"

Grandpa knocked the ashes from his pipe in an ashtray and put it down on the table. He reached over and patted my hand. I think he said, "There, there," but he said it so quietly, I couldn't be sure he had said anything at all.

I looked at him. The smoke from his pipe still floated up and half covered his face. Sometimes, other times when that happens, he looks at me from behind that cloud and smiles or winks at me, as if we had a private secret or something. But now he just looked funny, sort of sad, and he nodded at me a few times. All of a sudden I felt like crying and never stopping. Then the phone rang. I jumped up to answer it, to get away.

"Jeremy!" It was Mimi. She sounded all breathless, like she was excited or something. "Jeremy! Want to sleep over tonight?"

"I don't know," I said. "I guess. If I'm allowed." I tried to make my voice sound normal, so she wouldn't know I'd been crying. "What's up?"

"You'll see!" she said. "Hurry up—ask!"

I could hear her start to laugh. I turned from the phone. "Grandma? Can I sleep over at Mimi and Libby's tonight?"

Grandma looked at Grandpa, questioning. He nodded once.

"I'm allowed," I said into the phone. "But what's up?"

Mimi was really laughing now. "You'll see," she said.

2

Grandma made me eat some dinner first. Then I grabbed my sleeping bag and toothbrush and said good-bye as fast as I could. I ran down the steps and past the door of the store. Grandma and Grandpa live in an apartment over Grandpa's paint store. "Martin's Paints" it says out front, in big green letters.

I ran all the way to Mimi and Libby's house. I tried to pretend that Mom's letter had never come, that everything was just the same as it was this morning before I got the letter. But all the time I was running, I kept going over the words I would use when she called tomorrow. I thought if I could just find the right words to say, I could persuade her to change her mind and come home. Dad didn't need her as much as I did.

When I got to the twins' house, Mimi met me at the door before I could even ring the bell. She pulled me inside the hall, real quietly. "Shush!" she warned, putting her finger over her lips.

"Why?" I whispered back.

"Because. Carrie's upstairs."

"Carrie!" I practically screeched. "Why did you ask *Carrie*?"

"Shush!" Mimi said again. "Because I have a plan. Come here. I'll show you something."

She led the way to the dining room, then closed the

door behind us. She went over to a wood panel in the wall by the china closet and began tugging at it.

"What are you doing?"

"Shush!" Mimi hissed again, pointing to the closed door. "I don't want Mom to know. Or Carrie, either. Libby's trying to keep her out of our way for a minute."

Mimi kept pulling at the panel, prying it away from the wall. Finally it came off. Underneath was a door, and when Mimi pulled at the handle, it opened. It looked like a big box inside.

"Know what it is?" Mimi asked.

"No. What?" I whispered.

"A dumbwaiter!" Mimi said.

"A dumb what?"

"A dumbwaiter! They used to use it for sending things up and downstairs. Look!" She pointed to some ropes that looked like a pulley. "Give me your sleeping bag."

Mimi put it in the box and began pulling on the rope. I could see the box disappear, going slowly upward.

"Where's it going?" I said.

"Upstairs," Mimi said, "to my mother's room."

"Your mother's room!" I said. "How'm I going to get it back?" Mrs. Royce's room was the one place in the house where we weren't allowed to play.

"No problem," Mimi said. "Come on!"

She closed the dumbwaiter door, then pushed the panel back in place. We tiptoed out into the hall and ran up to Mrs. Royce's room.

It was dark in there. Mimi switched on a lamp and closed the door. She moved the dressing table aside, then began tugging on a panel in the wall, just like the one downstairs. She got it off, then reached into the hole and turned around.

"Ladies and gentlemen!" she announced. "I now present—for your pleasure—a beautiful—sleeping bag!" She pulled it out, and I grabbed it back from her.

"I tried to get into the dumbwaiter this afternoon," Mimi said, "but I couldn't. My legs are too long." She paused, giving me that look that she has sometimes when she expects me to know something.

"So?" I said.

"So," Mimi said. "Carrie's a shrimp. I'll bet she'll fit."

That sounded like fun, even if it was scary. "Let me try!" I said.

"No way," Mimi said. "If I don't fit, you won't."

I looked at her. She was right. I'm bigger than she is, even though we're the same age. But Carrie would fit. She really is a shrimp. She's our age, too, but she's practically a midget.

"Rats!" I said. "Wish I was Carrie!"

"No, you don't," Mimi said. She was smiling. "Not when you see what we do to her."

"What?"

"Well, first," Mimi said, "we tell her what fun it is to have a ride. We tell her we did it already. Then when she gets in, we send her upstairs—halfway up, not all the way. We stop it between floors—and we don't let her out!"

"That's mean!" I said, but I was laughing at the idea.

"I know," Mimi said. "But it's not half as mean—it's nothing—compared to what she did to us!"

"Yeah," I said.

I knew what Mimi meant. Last week, Carrie had gotten us into real trouble. The twins and I had gone into this big office building around the corner from Grandma's, where there are some doctor's offices. We got on the elevator and had fun zipping up to the eighteenth floor and back down again. Mimi had found a button you could push that said "Emergency Express." When you pushed it, the elevator didn't stop at any of the floors in between. We did that for about half an hour. When we finally got off, there was this huge crowd of really angry people waiting for the elevator. The doorman grabbed us by the elbows and walked us right out of the front door. When we got outside, we were really laughing, and we told some of the kids in the neighborhood about it. But when Carrie heard, she told her mother on us. And because Mrs. Wibler talks as much as Carrie does, she called the twins' mother and Grandma right away. For the whole rest of the day, Mimi and Libby and I were punished. We weren't allowed out or anything. Grandma wouldn't even let me go to the movie we had planned that night.

"Yeah," I said again and nodded. "Okay. It's not as mean as what she did to us. But you know what? She's going to scream her head off."

"I know," Mimi said. "But that's the other part I

didn't tell you about. My mother's going to a meeting tonight!"

"O–*kay!*" I said.

"And while she's gone, we'll give Carrie her own private 'Emergency Express' ride!" said Mimi gleefully.

"Mimi! Libby!" It was Mrs. Royce calling. "Are you there? Where are your friends?"

"Hurry!" Mimi said. "Get out of here!"

She pushed the panel back on quickly, and we ran out into the hall. We closed the door quietly behind us.

"Yes! We're here!" we both answered at once.

Libby and Carrie came out of Libby's room into the hall, too. Libby grinned at Mimi.

"Oh, you were so quiet," Mrs. Royce said. "I'm going to my meeting now, but I'll be back soon. Be good now." She paused. She looked funny, as though she had just thought of something. "You won't get into anything, will you?"

"I'll make sure they don't, Mrs. Royce," Carrie said sweetly. "I hope you have a nice meeting!"

Mrs. Royce smiled at her.

"Don't worry, Mom," Libby said. "*We* won't get into a thing!"

"Good!" Mrs. Royce smiled at us all, then turned and went out the front door.

Mimi waited just a second. Then she ran downstairs and locked the door. She called upstairs. "Hey, Carrie! Come here! Wait'll we show you what we found!"

We all ran downstairs into the dining room. Carrie

went over to where Mimi was pulling at the cover on the wall. "What is it?" she said. Even her voice was small. She sounded like a mouse.

"Look!" Mimi said triumphantly, pulling off the panel.

Carrie peered into the opening. "Boy!" she squeaked. "A dumbwaiter! I didn't know you had one!"

We all stared at her, our mouths open.

"How'd you know it was a dumbwaiter?" Libby asked after a minute. She sounded really disgusted.

"My grandma has one. We use it all the time!" Carrie said. "Once, when my uncle was little, my grandma said he put the cat on the dumbwaiter." Carrie kept talking. Once she got started, she talked forever. "And the dumbwaiter broke, and the cat got stuck down inside the wall. It took three days to get him out, and nobody couldn't sleep or anything, listening to that cat cry!" Carrie laughed. It was just like her to laugh at some poor cat stuck in a wall.

Mimi, Libby, and I just looked at one another. We could see our plan fast disappearing.

"Well, this one doesn't break," Mimi said quickly. "I tried it this afternoon, so we know it works. Libby gave me a ride."

"Really?" Carrie squeaked. "Bet you were scared."

"Bet I wasn't," Mimi said. "It was neat! It was just like the fun house I went into at a carnival once." She began putting the cover back on the wall.

"Hey, Mimi," Libby said suddenly, as if she had just thought of it. "We ought to let Carrie have a turn."

"No way!" Mimi said. "She'd probably break it. Besides, she'd be too scared."

"I would not be scared!" Carrie said. "And I don't weigh as much as you do."

"You would too be scared," Mimi said. "Remember how scared you were this morning when we were exploring in that other place?"

"That was different." Carrie shivered. "My mother says there's rats down there!"

"So, maybe there's rats in the wall," Mimi said.

Carrie screamed.

"Come on, Mimi," I said. "You know there's no rats in the wall! Let's let Carrie have a turn. She won't break it. She's littler than you."

Mimi looked at Carrie really carefully, as though she were measuring her.

Carrie looked back as if she were holding her breath, waiting for Mimi to say yes.

"Okay," Mimi said, finally. "But just once."

"O—*kay!*" Carrie squealed and clapped her hands.

We tried a couple ways to get Carrie into the dumbwaiter. I wondered when she would begin to think it funny that we didn't know how to do it, but she never said anything. Finally, she found a way. She backed in, sat down, pulled her knees up, and wrapped her arms tight around them.

"Let's go!" she said.

"Okay." Mimi said. "Up you go. See you upstairs!" She began pulling on the rope. The dumbwaiter and Carrie disappeared up into the wall.

"Go on upstairs!" Mimi ordered Libby in a whisper. "Tell me when you can see the top of this thing."

Libby and I ran upstairs.

"Okay!" Libby yelled, looking into the hole.

Mimi must have stopped pulling then because the dumbwaiter stopped. She came running into the room and put one finger over her lips. We all stood around the opening in the wall.

"Hey!" Carrie squeaked after a minute. "Hey! This thing stopped!"

We didn't say anything. We looked at one another and started to laugh.

"Hey!" she yelled again. "It's stuck! Let me out! Let me out!"

We were all laughing. Carrie was really screaming.

After a minute, I said, "We better let her out. She won't be able to breathe."

Carrie was shouting at the top of her lungs. "She doesn't sound like she can't breathe," Mimi said. "Besides, the cat could breathe for three days."

"Mi-mi!" I said.

"All right, all right," she said. She went over to the dumbwaiter and began yanking at the pulley. "Just a minute," she called to Carrie. "It just takes a minute. I forgot to tell you that."

Mimi tugged at the pulley. "Un—uh!" she grunted. She pulled at it some more, all the while making sounds as if she were really working hard.

"Hurry up, Mimi!" Libby whispered. "Stop faking!"

"I'm not faking!" Mimi said. She wiped her hands on her pants. She pulled at the ropes again. She turned around. "It won't move!" Her face was really pale and her eyes were wide. "I mean it! It won't move!"

"Let me try it," Libby said.

Mimi moved over, and Libby took her place at the wall. She pulled and grunted, but nothing happened.

Libby turned around. "It's really stuck," she whispered. She looked as if she was about to cry.

Carrie was wailing again. "Let me out! Let me out!"

"Listen," I said to Mimi and Libby, "go downstairs and try it."

"It worked this afternoon from up here," Libby said.

"Try it anyway," I said. "I'll stay up here and see if I can work it from this end."

Mimi and Libby raced downstairs. I went back to the dumbwaiter. "Just a minute!" I called to Carrie.

"What's the matter?" Carrie cried. "Pull me up! My legs hurt! They're asleep! They're all numb! And so's my bottom!"

"Well, you'll be out in a minute."

I could see the dumbwaiter begin to shake a little as Mimi and Libby pulled at it from downstairs. All of a sudden, it began to move slowly.

"Is it moving?" Mimi called.

"A little," I answered. I could reach down and touch the top of it now. "A little more!" I called.

"It won't move any more," Mimi called.

I yanked at the pulley. The dumbwaiter shot up into

the opening. At the same time I heard a big snap as if something broke. I screamed, expecting the dumb-waiter to go crashing down, but it stayed where it was.

I reached in. I was so afraid for Carrie I practically pulled her out. She was cramped up like a pretzel. Her arms were twisted up around her legs, and she could hardly stand.

"I'm going to tell my mother on you!" she sobbed as I pulled her out.

I felt like stuffing her back in.

"I'm going to tell Mimi's mother, too!" she screamed. She stood up then and wobbled toward the stairs. She was really screaming now. "I'm going home to get my mother this minute! I'm going to get my mother! She's going to come over here—*right now!*"

3

It took us half the night to calm Carrie down, and we had to promise her practically the whole world before she agreed not to tell her mother or Mrs. Royce. But just "for now—ow!" she said. That's the way she said it, "Now—ow." She sounded like a cat.

I promised to give her all the post cards with pictures of castles that my mom had sent from London all summer. And Mimi had to give away her ring, the one with the gray stone and the picture of a sea gull painted on it that she got at Cape Cod last summer. And Libby had to do the worst thing of all. She had to promise to play with Carrie every day for a whole week!

The next day, Mimi and I stayed as far away from Libby as possible because she was with Carrie. We felt like rats, but I wouldn't have played with Carrie if somebody had given me a million dollars.

Carrie's a pain. Except for her, it's been great here at Grandma's this summer. I've had lots of fun with Mimi and Libby. They're identical twins, and hardly anyone can tell them apart, but they sure *act* different. Libby's quiet, and she's scared of a lot of the things that Mimi likes to do. Mimi's just the opposite. She's hardly scared of anything, and she gets all the good ideas, even if she sometimes gets us in trouble because of them.

But Carrie! I tried to like Carrie when I first came here, but she makes it very hard. Even the way she looks is disgusting. She's a shrimp. Her hands are so tiny. They're all pink and shiny. I touched them once, and they're so soft they almost feel slippery. But the worst thing about her is the way she tells her mother about everything. About everybody!

I played with Mimi all day, but I knew Mom was calling at six o'clock, so at five-thirty I went back to Grandma's.

Grandma was in the kitchen making dinner when I came in, and she started fussing. "Jeremy!" she said. "Where have you been? It's almost six o'clock!"

I looked at the clock. "It's five-thirty!" I said.

"That's *almost* six o'clock!" Grandma said. "You might have missed that call!"

My grandma's always worrying about being late. She wakes me up two hours before I have to be somewhere, and I get there half an hour too early anyway. On Sundays, we always have to sit in church by ourselves and wait twenty minutes before anyone else even shows up.

"I'm sorry," I said. I knew there wasn't any sense in arguing with her.

"Oh, it's all right," Grandma said. She came over to me, smoothed my hair, and twisted a piece of it around her finger, trying to get it out of my face. "It's not your fault," she said. "I'm just all edgy these days. Maybe it's the heat or something."

I nodded. I felt all edgy, too. Together we began to set the table. Grandma got out the white tablecloth she uses at night and the plates and silverware. All the while, I kept rehearsing what I was going to say to Mom. If I could just say the right words, then maybe I could get her to change her mind and come home.

When the phone rang, I grabbed it. I had to wait while the operator said some things, but then I heard my mother's voice. She sounded so close, as if she were practically in the same room!

"Jeremy!" she said. "Honey! Is that you?"

"It's me!" I said. "Where are you?"

She laughed. "In London, of course!"

"Oh," I said. Now that I could finally talk to her, I felt funny, like I didn't know what to say.

"How are you, honey?" Mom said.

"Fine," I said. "Thank you."

My mom laughed, that funny, deep laugh she has that makes me feel so good. "Nothing to say, love? Then I'll talk first—while you think."

I took a deep breath and smiled. Mom really understands sometimes.

She started to talk, telling me about what she and Daddy were doing and about my father's business. She told me about going to Kensington Gardens and the palace and watching the changing of the guards. "We have lots of pictures to show you," Mom said. "Lots and lots. And next year, we'll come back and take you.

And when we do, maybe we'll stay at the Savoy again. There's a tub in our bathroom that's almost as big as a swimming pool!"

"Wow!" I said. "When am I going?"

Mom laughed. "Next year, darling. Next year."

"I know," I said. "I just wondered. How's Daddy?"

"He's right here," Mom said. "He wants to talk to you, too. But first. . . ." My mother paused. She sounded funny all of a sudden, as if maybe she felt shy, too. "But first, Jeremy, you do understand about our having to stay on here, don't you? You did get our letter, didn't you?"

"Yes," I said. "But—"

"Good," Mom said. "You know, Jeremy, it's awfully important to Daddy. It's a real opportunity for him—maybe a promotion. It's only a few more months."

I began to get this feeling in my stomach, this weird feeling I get when I'm scared. I knew I had to say quick what I was going to say, what I had practiced. I started to talk, really fast.

"Jeremy," Mom interrupted. "Listen to me, honey. It's really important. You understand, don't you? You can go to school with all your new friends. Grandma tells me you've made lots of new friends!"

For a minute I didn't answer. I couldn't! It was actually happening, and I couldn't even say anything!

"Jeremy," Mom was saying. "You wrote you were having fun there."

My stomach began to hurt, like I was really getting sick. How could she do this?

"I can't!" I said finally. Those weren't the words I had practiced, but it was all I could think of. I began to cry. "Why don't *you* come home?" I said. "Daddy can stay there by himself!"

"We thought about that, darling," Mom said. "But you know how Daddy relies on me for help. And since it's such a short time, we think it's better this way. You'll do fine there. It's only until Christmas."

"Christmas?" I said. "Christmas! That's forever!"

"It probably seems that way, darling," Mom said. "But believe me, it will come before you know it."

"But I can't!" I said. "I can't go to school here!"

"Of course you can, dear," Mom said. She was beginning to use that supersensible voice she uses whenever she's trying to get me to do something.

"Why can't you, sweetheart?" she said when I didn't answer her. "With all your new friends and—"

"You *know* why not!" I said. I was getting mad. I wouldn't say it out loud. She already knew. She just wanted me to say it so she could say, "You'll be fine, dear. All you have to do is take your pills." That's all she ever says about it.

"Jeremy," Mom said. "You're going to be fine, you know."

There! I didn't even have to say it. It seemed as though she wasn't even talking to me, as though she were a record or something.

"Jeremy," Mom said. "I knew you'd be awfully disappointed. But you're going to do fine. Believe me. You take your medicine, and everything's going to be fine. Now, you'll feel better in a little while. Would you like to talk to Daddy?"

I nodded because I couldn't talk.

"All right?" she said.

"All right," I said. I tried to make my voice sound normal. I didn't want to cry.

"Jeremy?" Mom said. "Remember Baby Bear?"

"Yes." I remembered Baby Bear. When I was very little, my mom and I used to pretend there was this little bear called Baby Bear who came into my room at night, and he used to leave me presents and stuff. But we both knew it was really my mom.

"Jeremy," Mom said softly. "Baby Bear misses you."

"Uh-hunh," I said. I was trying so hard not to cry that I was practically choking. I could hardly speak. "Bye," I whispered.

My dad came on the phone, and we talked for a minute, and then I hung up. I held back my tears long enough to say good night to Grandma and Grandpa, then I ran into my room and closed the door. I really started to cry then. Why didn't I tell Mom I missed her, too? Maybe—maybe even—I'd been crying so hard —maybe she didn't even hear me say, "Good-bye!"

I got undressed, climbed into bed, and pulled up the sheets. The door opened a crack. It was Grandma.

"To bed so early, honey? No dinner?" she asked. "Do you feel all right?"

"Yes, I'm just tired," I said.

"Sleep well then," she said and closed the door.

I began to cry again. I couldn't go to school here.

Why couldn't Mom and Dad understand that? Didn't they know I couldn't let it happen again?

All of a sudden, I got this picture in my mind of when it happened at my other school. I could see all the kids standing around, looking down, staring at me, laughing. I sat up in bed, squeezed my eyes closed, and pressed hard against my eyeballs with my fingers. That made all shiny spots come and the picture disappeared.

I felt bad because I knew I was being selfish, crying like this and all. But it was just that it was so *important*. Couldn't they see that? I didn't mean to think only of myself. I knew Mom and Daddy had their own problems, that Daddy's business is important, that they have needs, too. But why couldn't they think about *my* needs, *my* problems?

What if it happened? What if I got sick here? They don't know what it's like. *They* don't have epilepsy.

4

When I woke up it was morning. I felt as if I had cried all night, but I must have fallen asleep. I could smell something baking. I sat up. Muffins! Grandma must have made me some muffins! I got up and dressed and went out to the kitchen.

"Well, good morning," Grandma said. "You're up early." She had that look she gets when she's worried.

I tried to smile back. I knew Grandma was trying to make me feel better and that's why she made me the muffins.

When I sat down at the table, I looked at Grandpa. He didn't look worried, the way Grandma did. But he raised his eyebrows at me a little, as though he was asking me a question or something, as though he wanted to know what I was thinking. I looked away. I couldn't talk about anything right then.

I was surprised when I started to eat. Last night, I had thought I'd never eat again in my life. But now, all of a sudden, I was really hungry. I ate about four muffins and was just starting on another when there was a knock on the door—Mimi!

I saw Grandma wince, the way she always does when Mimi knocks. Mimi knocks the way nobody else does, as if she's trying to knock the door down.

Grandpa smiled at me, that little smile. "Your friends are out early," he said.

I nodded and quickly went to the door.

"Jeremy!" Somebody was standing at the door, but for a minute I couldn't tell who it was.

"Mimi?" I said. Her face was covered with mud, and so were her clothes.

"Jeremy!" Mimi said. "Come on! Wait'll we show you what we found!"

I looked over my shoulder at Grandma. I stood in the middle of the doorway and hoped she couldn't see Mimi. "Grandma?" I said. "Can I go out? I'll do my chores later."

Grandma shook her head as if she were saying no, but then she said, "All right. I guess so. But, Jeremy, please try to stay clean." She smiled. "We're going shopping this afternoon. Grandpa wants to buy you something pretty to wear to school next week."

I looked at Grandpa. "Thanks," I said.

He just waved his pipe at me. "Git!" he said.

I ran downstairs with Mimi. Libby was waiting at the bottom. She was almost as dirty as Mimi.

"Where've you two *been*?" I said. "Where are we going?"

"Woodfield!" Mimi said. "Hurry up!" We started to run.

Woodfield is the place where we had been the other day, trying to get the cover off a manhole. We play there a lot. There's a big empty building that used to be an orphanage or something, and it has a field and some trees around it.

When we got to Woodfield, Mimi and Libby ran

right over to the manhole. They started pulling at the cover. They were both grunting, and their faces got really red. But all of a sudden, the cover came off.

"How'd you do that?" I said.

"It wasn't locked down!" Mimi said. "In fact, when we first came here this morning, it was off! Somebody must have worked down there yesterday and forgot to put it back on."

"Did you go down?" I said.

"Are you kidding?" Mimi shook her head at me. "Of course we went down, dummy! Come on! Let's go!" She was sitting on the side of the hole, her feet dangling down inside. "You coming?" she said to Libby.

I looked at Libby. She was standing off to the side, looking really grouchy.

"What's the matter?" I said.

"It's disgusting down there," she said.

"Come on, Lib," Mimi said. She always calls her that when she's trying to get her to do something. "Remember what we found?"

"What'd you find?" I said.

"Lots of things," Mimi said. "Right, Lib?"

"Right," Libby said, but she still sounded grouchy. "Promise we won't stay down long?"

"Promise!" Mimi said. "Five minutes!"

We all climbed into the hole. There was a long ladder down with iron rungs, really far apart. My legs could just reach from one rung to the next. At the bottom, I had to drop a long way to the ground.

It was pitch dark and smelled awful, sort of like wet dog fur. Under my sneakers, the ground was all soft and squishy.

"C'mon," Mimi said. She switched on a flashlight.

"Where'd you get that?" I asked.

"Oh, I have ways," Mimi said. She started to walk away.

I followed, and Libby came after me. It was so dark I could hardly see, except where Mimi was holding the flashlight. There were sounds everywhere.

"What are the noises?" I whispered. I didn't know why I was whispering, but I had the feeling someone was watching us.

"I don't know," Mimi said. She didn't sound at all scared.

The noises seemed to get louder, and I could feel the ground shaking. I stopped short, and Libby almost walked up my back. "It's water!" I shouted. I had the feeling someone would flush a toilet someplace and water would come rushing in all around us. I turned around to run, but Libby was still right behind me.

"Stop it, Jeremy!" Mimi grabbed my shirt. "There's no water down here—N-O—water! Honest! We were here a long time this morning. Now, c'mon! It's fun when you get out under the street. You can hear cars and stuff over your head."

I followed her a long way, turning lots of corners. We could hear water dripping once, but the other sounds weren't so bad any more.

"Now, listen," Mimi said.

We stopped. All of a sudden the sound came again, this time right next to me. It got louder and louder. The ground began to shake. At the same time, the light went out.

"Mimi!" I shouted. I reached out to grab her—but she was gone. My hands touched a wall of wet earth. I felt up and down it. I was at the end of the tunnel, and Mimi was gone! I turned around for Libby. I reached out again, but I only touched air.

"Yah!" Somebody shouted, right at my shoulder. I screamed. It was Mimi. She turned the flashlight back on.

She and Libby were both leaning against a wall, all bent over because they were laughing so hard. I didn't think it was funny, and I turned my back on them, but I could only stare at the stupid dirt wall.

"That's not funny," I said. I had to bite my lip to keep from crying.

"Ah, Jeremy!" Mimi said. "I was only teasing. Look, the tunnel makes a turn here. I just hid around the corner. And the noise is only the subway. Isn't that neat? When a train goes by, it makes the ground shake. We don't have to go any farther if you don't want to."

"It's not that I don't *want* to," I said. "I'm just scared to death."

"Yeah," Mimi said. "I was scared, too—at first. But isn't it fun? Nobody knows where we are. We could stay here forever if we wanted to!"

I didn't think that would be much fun.

Mimi pointed to this little wall, sort of like a shelf, that stuck out right where we were standing. "Sit down there," she said. "And I'll show you the best part. But you have to be quiet—really, really quiet—and we'll see some rats!"

"I don't *want* to see some rats!" Libby said, before I could say it. "I told you that!"

"Oh, Lib, they're not going to bother you," Mimi said. "Now shush."

"They're already 'bothering' me," Libby said. "And I'm not going to shush. I'm going to keep on talking, and I'm going to bang my feet, too, and make all the noise I can to keep them away!"

"You might step on one," Mimi said.

Libby screamed and pulled her feet up under her.

Mimi turned to me. "Wait'll you see them," she said. Her eyes were really wide. "They're the biggest rats you've ever seen. And they look right at you, like they're not even scared. It's really exciting!"

Libby was staring at Mimi. "You'd think she just discovered America," she said. She stood up. "I'm getting out of here."

"Hope you don't get lost," Mimi said.

Libby gave her sister a dirty look, but then she sat back down.

We were quiet for a few minutes when Mimi poked me. "Look! There!" She pointed.

Something was moving along the tunnel toward us. I pulled my feet under me, too. "Is that a rat?" I whispered.

"Sure, it's a rat," Mimi said. "I told you they were big."

It was huge, almost as big as a cat even. It had a long, pointy nose, and whiskers, and it kept wiggling them while it walked. Only its tail looked like what I thought a rat's tail should look like—long and thin and pointy, like the "rattail" combs my grandma has.

It came right up practically to our feet and stood there, looking.

I held my breath and looked back. Could rats climb up ledges, or jump?

Mimi whispered to me, "Think I could touch him?"

I stared at her. "That's gross! Besides, don't they bite?"

"Nah. I wouldn't touch his head. Just his tail. Watch!"

Mimi handed me the flashlight. She crawled off the ledge, very slowly, as if she were in a trance. Libby and I held our breaths. Mimi was only about a foot away from the rat. She crouched down so slowly, she hardly looked like she was moving at all. The rat backed up a little. Mimi stopped moving. The rat took a step forward again. Its nose and whiskers were twitching, and its round, beady eyes were fixed on Mimi. It crept forward a little, staying close to the wall. Mimi's hand was moving out slowly. The rat looked at her for a minute; then very slowly it turned around and began moving down the tunnel, back along the way it had come.

Mimi moved fast. She took one quick step after him, bent over, and stuck out her hand like lightning.

"I did it!" she screamed. "I did it! Look!"

She plopped back on the ledge and grabbed my hand, as if by feeling it I could tell that she had just touched a rat.

I screamed and pulled away.

Libby was screaming, too. "You did not touch him! You did not!"

"Did, too!" Mimi was laughing.

I stood up. "C'mon! Let's get out of here!" I grabbed Libby's hand and pulled her behind me, and I pushed Mimi ahead. They went, but they were still fighting.

"You didn't come within a mile of him!" Libby called to her sister over my shoulder.

"You're full of it," Mimi called back. "I touched him, and you saw me!"

When we turned a corner, it was pitch dark, even with the flashlight. I was still holding Libby's hand. Mimi reached for mine, but I said, "No, thanks." I didn't know which hand she had touched the rat with, so I held her shoulder instead.

Mimi began to sing. "Oh, if I had a nickel, I'd buy us all a pickle."

I joined in. We marched to the tune. Even Libby sang. I think she forgot that she might step on a rat.

After a few minutes, I stopped singing. It seemed to me as if we should be back to the manhole by now. I wondered if Mimi had noticed, too.

"Mimi?" I said quietly. "Are we lost?"

"Nah," she said. "We'll be there in a minute."

We walked some more. We had all stopped singing.

"We've passed this place at least twice," Libby said at last.

"How do you know?" Mimi said. "All these places look the same."

"Not to me they don't," Libby said.

"Me, neither," I said. "I think we passed the subway at least twice."

"Look!" Libby said. She pointed. "There's the wall where we sat!"

She was right! We were right back where we started from, back to the wall where we sat and watched the rat. We must have come all the way around in a circle!

"Oh, wow!" Mimi plopped against the wall.

I looked at Libby. I wondered if she was going to start to cry.

I remembered what Mimi had said before: "Nobody knows where we are. We could stay here forever!" I thought *I* would start to cry. I thought about my mom and dad. It would serve them right if I got lost down here forever. Then they'd be sorry they didn't come back!

We were all quiet for a while. I began to be cold, inside and out. Finally I said a little prayer inside. "God," I said, "I'll go to school here if you'll just get us out of this place." I stood up. "Look," I said. "If we got in here, then we can get out—right?"

Nobody answered me. They just stared.

"Right?" I said again.

They still didn't answer.

I grabbed their hands and pulled them up. "Come on!" I said. "Let's try again. Only, Mimi, every time we come to a corner, you hold the flashlight and shine it around. And, Libby, you and I'll feel around and see if there's more than one way to go. If there's two ways, we try them both. One of them has to be the right one!"

They still didn't say anything, but we started out again. At each corner, we felt all around, but each time there was only one way to go. I got more and more scared. I didn't care if it did serve my parents right; I didn't want to be lost down here forever.

We came to another corner, but there was only one way to go, and we started out again.

"Wait!" It was Libby. "Wait a minute!"

I turned around. She wasn't behind me any more. "Where are you?"

"Here!" she said. Her voice sounded far away.

"Where?"

"Over here! Mimi! Shine the light over here!"

Mimi swung the flashlight in a big circle. We could see Libby a little way away to the side.

"There's a tunnel here!" she said. To prove it, she disappeared around a corner. "And there's light down here!"

We both started to run. We were tripping over each

other trying to get to the hole at the same time. Around the corner, we could see sunlight!

At the bottom of the manhole, we took turns boosting and pulling each other up to the first rung. I was last out and took half the skin off my shin.

Back up in the sun, we flopped down on the grass.

"Wow!" Mimi said after we'd all caught our breath again. "Next time we better take bigger flashlights!"

"*Next* time?" Libby screeched. "I wouldn't go down there again in a million years! And look at us! How're we going to get all this gunk off?"

I looked at Mimi and Libby and at myself. We were filthy. We looked disgusting. Suddenly I remembered what Grandma had said about staying clean.

"Oh, man!" I said. "Am I in trouble!"

Mimi smiled. She had that "I've got a plan" look again.

"Forget it!" I said before she could say anything. I had had enough of Mimi's plans. I stood up. "I'm going home. See you later."

I ran home, praying all the way that I could get in before Grandma saw me.

When I went by the store, I peeked in. Grandpa was in there, but I didn't see Grandma. I hoped she was back in the laundry or something. I opened the door to the apartment and went upstairs very quietly.

I opened the kitchen door and almost knocked Grandma over! She was standing right behind the door, washing a window.

"Jeremy!" she said when she saw me. "Jeremy Martin! I told you to stay clean!" She shook her head and stared. Then she said really slowly and softly, "Where were you, anyway? You look like you've been in a *sewer!*"

5

Grandma was really angry—at first. To make it worse, I felt like laughing, and she could tell. It was only because of what she said about the sewer. If she only knew! But I took a quick bath and put all my things in the washer, so Grandma got over her mad pretty fast.

When we went shopping, I got a super new dress for school. It was light blue and really puffy with lace on the top, and the skirt spun way out every time I turned around. I think Grandma thought it was too dressy for school, but Grandpa said I could have whatever I wanted, and I really loved that dress.

When we got home, I wanted to go over to Mimi and Libby's. I decided to tell them about going to school here. I hadn't said anything about it in the morning because I had been afraid they'd ask why and that I might start crying again. I hoped now they wouldn't ask too many questions.

When I got to their house, Mimi and Libby were in the kitchen. Libby was sitting on a counter and Mimi was sitting cross-legged in the middle of the kitchen table. I didn't see their mother anywhere.

"Did your mom see you when you got home?" I asked.

"Nah," Mimi said. "We just waited till she went down to the store."

"Lucky!" I said.

Mr. Royce owns a drugstore, and it has a counter where you can eat. Every day at noon, Mrs. Royce goes to the store to help serve lunch.

"I ran right into Grandma," I said.

"Yikes!" Libby said. "What'd she say?"

"She said I looked like I'd been in a sewer."

Libby screamed.

Mimi laughed so hard she almost fell off the table. "What'd you say to that?" she said, when she finished laughing.

"Nothing. I just took a bath—fast."

"Wow!" Libby said. "Here!" She handed me the peanut butter jar. "Want some?"

I took the peanut butter and started making a sandwich. I looked at the sandwiches Mimi and Libby were making. They both had peanut butter, too, but Mimi was slicing fat slices of bananas all over hers. And Libby was cutting little tiny pieces of cheddar cheese and making designs of it all over hers.

"You two are gross!" I said. "Why don't you just use jelly on your peanut butter like normal people do?"

"'Cause we're not normal," Mimi said. "We're weird!" She made a face and twisted up her hand like a claw. "I'm Andrew Malin," she groaned.

"Who's Andrew Malin?" I said.

"Kid in our class," Mimi said. "He's weird. He's got a funny disease that makes him walk like he's drunk."

I ate my sandwich quietly for a moment.

"I'm going to be in your class," I said finally.

"What!" Mimi screamed.

"What?" Libby screeched.

They were both staring at me.

"You're kidding!" Libby said.

"Nope."

"How come?" Mimi said.

" 'Cause my mom and dad haven't finished their business in London yet. Won't for a couple months, so—"

"O—kay! O—kay!" Mimi was shouting. She jumped down from the table and went over to Libby. She grabbed her arm and leaned over her and whispered something in her ear.

"All—right!" Libby said, real slowly.

They both turned around and stared at me. Libby's eyes were wide and Mimi was grinning, but it was a funny smile. She looked like she had just done something really awful.

"Want to hear a secret?" Mimi said softly.

"Secret?" I said. I didn't know why, but all of a sudden I felt hot and nervous. They didn't mean a secret—like my secret, did they?

"Do you?" Mimi said. "Do you want to see something?"

"Sure," I said, even though I wasn't.

"Come on!" Mimi grabbed my arm and practically pulled me out of the room.

We ran up to their bedroom. Mimi went right over to the dresser. She pulled out the bottom drawer and dumped everything on the floor—socks and T-shirts and some rolled-up stiff bathing suits. Then she turned the drawer upside down.

Taped to the bottom of it, with fat strips of masking tape, was a blue, spiral notebook.

"Wow!" I said. "What a neat hiding place!"

Mimi looked happy. "Betsy did that in the *Mystery of the Blue Skull*," she said.

Very carefully, she pulled off the tape, took the book off, and opened it. Inside was a list of all the kids in her and Libby's class. There was a page for each one. Some pages had only a name and a couple things about the kid. Other pages were crammed with stuff. When I read it, at first I didn't believe some of the things, but Mimi and Libby swore they were all true.

First, there was Andrew Malin—"WEIRDO." He wore a baseball cap all the time, and for some reason the teacher even let him wear it in class. But one day, Mimi knocked the cap off—accidentally—and everybody could see that Andrew was bald. And then there was Jay Carson, whose head was round like a basketball who wore the same shirt every day for two weeks without changing it, and who smelled rancid. And there was Julia Monaghan, who had a great big mouth and huge teeth, and when she smiled, she tried to hide her teeth, and then you could only see her gums.

Carrie had five pages. All of them were filled. One page was a list of everything she ate for lunch last term. Mimi and Libby kept a record because they wanted to find out why she was so skinny. Every day was the same. Carrie ate one half of one half of a sandwich, one bite of apple or something, and three sips of milk.

"No wonder she's so skinny!" I said. "Is that really *all* she ate?"

"Yup!" Mimi said. "Except for one day. We told her we were starting a club and she couldn't join unless she ate all her lunch. So that day she ate everything. It took her the whole lunchtime, recess and all, and I stayed in the cafeteria and watched, and she really did. She ate everything!"

"So, did you let her join?" I said.

"Nope," Mimi said. "Right before school was out that afternoon, she went in the lavatory and threw it all up. So we told her it didn't count."

I laughed, but I thought to myself that that was sort of mean.

"What's this?" I said. I had turned a page of the notebook, and all it said was: "Mr. Frackhorn—Nervous Breakdown—February 5."

Mimi and Libby both started to laugh. "That was our teacher," Libby said.

"Did he really have a breakdown?"

"Almost," Libby said. "We kept changing seats—I mean, Mimi and I did. He didn't know who was who. Once I sat in Mimi's place for a whole week and she sat at my desk. And he kept staring at us and staring at us. And when he finally thought he knew who was me and who was Mimi, we changed back again."

I laughed.

"I cried!" Mimi said.

"Cried?" Somehow I couldn't picture Mimi crying over that.

"Yeah," Mimi said. "It got him all upset. I used to pretend it really hurt my feelings when he called me Libby by mistake. So that week when we changed places, I let him call me Libby all week, and when we changed back, I burst into tears. And so did he—almost! He ran out of the room and didn't come back!"

"Did he ever come back?" I said.

"Not for the rest of the week," Mimi said. "We had to have a substitute."

"Tell me more." I was beginning to feel nervous again. "What's the school like?"

"Oh, it's okay," Libby said. "Normal school. Bor-ing."

"Yeah," I said. "But like what?"

"*Told* you," Libby said. "Boring. Kids okay. Teachers?" She turned her hand this way and then that, as though she were weighing something. "Some good, some not so good. I don't know who we're having this year. Somebody said it was a new teacher."

"Su-per!" Mimi said. "I love new teachers! They don't know what they're doing." She looked at Libby for a minute. "Hey, Lib! Guess who we have to make a new page for?"

"Who?" I said. But I knew who.

"You!" they both said together.

"Why me?" I didn't think I wanted a page about me.

"'Cause you're going to be in our class, aren't you?" Mimi said. "So you have to have your own page."

I felt funny—sort of worried. I mean, even though they're best friends, what would they say? "So—go ahead," I said, as if I didn't care. I turned around and flopped down on the bed.

"Not with you here, dummy!" Mimi said. "You can never do it when the person's around! We'll do it later. Then we'll show it to you."

"Great," I thought! But I didn't say anything out loud.

"We'll do it tonight," Mimi said. "You can see it when it's finished." She looked at Libby, then smiled. "We'll write down everything we can think of. You don't have to worry so much. At least you're not weird!"

I swallowed hard, then I laughed.

6

It was a couple days before school started, the day before Labor Day, that I woke up early. Outside, it was foggy, and everything in the city was wet and dripping. I lay in bed, listening to the sounds and thinking. School was starting in a few days. My parents weren't coming back. I was going to have to go to school here. Still, I felt pretty good. It wasn't that I had completely stopped worrying about what might happen. It was just that Mimi and Libby made things sound kind of fun. They were crazy, but I liked them. I'd never had friends like them before, and I'd never done things at home like I did here.

I felt scared, though, when I thought about that, and a little guilty, too. Scared, because if Grandma found out some of the things we've been doing, I'd be in really big trouble. Guilty, because Grandma was letting me get away with murder because I pretended I was still feeling bad about my parents not coming back. She was letting me do things I'd never be allowed to do otherwise. Like today—Grandma knows I can't swim, but she was letting me go with Mimi and Libby on the bus to the beach. By ourselves! She'd never have let me do *that* a few weeks ago.

I must have fallen asleep again. When I woke up next, the sun was out, and the fog and mist were all drying up. I got dressed in about ten seconds, gulped down my breakfast, and said good-bye to Grandma.

Grandpa was reading the Sunday papers and smoking his pipe when I bent down to kiss him good-bye. He took the pipe out of his mouth and looked at me seriously. "Now take it easy," he said, so quietly I knew that Grandma couldn't hear him from across the room. "You be careful. The beach is no place for wild stuff."

I looked at him. I wondered if he knew some of the things we'd been doing. "I'll be careful," I promised him. I grabbed my things and ran downstairs.

Mimi and Libby were at the bus stop, waiting for me. I could see they were wearing their swim team bathing suits, and they had T-shirts on top of them.

"Took you long enough," Mimi said when she saw me.

"I just woke up," I said. "What do you have?"

Mimi was holding something carefully in her hands. It looked like a comic book, but it was all wrapped up in waxed paper.

"It's the notebook," Mimi said. Then she laughed. "We have your page ready."

I swallowed hard. I pretended not to care too much, but I felt nervous again. "Why's it wrapped up like that?" I asked.

"Didn't want my mom to see it," Mimi said. "So I put it in the comic book. And I wrapped it up so it wouldn't get wet."

"Smart," I said. I was surprised. I'd never seen Mimi be so careful about anything before. I guesssed this notebook was pretty important to her. I waited until I could see the bus coming and we were getting our bags and towels together. "So, what'd you write about me?" I asked, as casually as I could.

"Don't worry. We'll show you," Mimi said. "When we're on the bus. It's not bad. Right, Libby?"

"Right," Libby said. It was the first thing Libby'd said so far. She looked unhappy.

The bus came, and we got on. We found a seat in the back. It smelled awful there, with all the smoke and exhaust from the bus, but it was the only place the three of us could sit together. When we sat down, Mimi unwrapped the book and handed it to me, open to my page.

"Here's you," she said.

I could feel my heart pounding hard. I put my face down so they couldn't see, and took a deep breath. I read:

Jeremy Martin:
Hair: sort of blond, sort of striped.
Eyes: blue.
Pretty.
Funny.
Personality: good.
Favorite clothes: dirty jeans, orange sneakers.
Best thing about her: Weird sense of humor.
Worst thing: Chicken.

"What?" I said. I almost screamed it. I couldn't help it. I hadn't meant to say anything at all, but when I read 'chicken,' I was mad! "What do you mean, 'chicken'?" I said.

"*Told* you, Mimi!" Libby said.

"Well, she is!" Mimi said. "Sometimes. Not all the time, but sometimes." She turned to me. "You're more chicken than *not* chicken. And I had to be honest!"

"Oh, yeah? Really? Who helped you get Carrie into the dumbwaiter? Who went with you into the sewer? Who helped you find your way *out* of the sewer when you were so *dumb* you got lost? Who sat there while you played with that stupid rat?"

"You did!" Mimi said. "I never said you didn't! But you can't say you weren't scared!" She looked at me as if she was waiting for me to say it.

"So," I said. "I was scared. A little. And so were you. That doesn't make me chicken!"

Mimi shrugged. "Can't help it," she said. "That's what I think. And I write the notebook!"

"Okay!" I said. "Great! So when do I get to do a page about you?"

"Sometime," Mimi said. She shrugged.

"You're scared," I said. "You don't want me to do it. You don't want to see what I write about you! Cause *you're* chicken! You should have seen your face when we got lost in the sewer. You looked like you'd just seen a ghost! You're just scared of what I'd write!"

"Am not!" Mimi said. "You can do it any time you want." She reached over and took the book away. "You're getting it all sweaty," she said.

I let her take the book away. "Tough on you," I thought! But I didn't say it out loud. "I'll show you who's chicken!"

We hardly said anything after that for the rest of the time on the bus. I stared out the window. I think Mimi stared straight ahead, but I didn't look at her much, so I couldn't be sure.

After a while, Libby started talking to me, telling me about the beach. I'd never been there, but they go there lots. Their mother lets them because they're really good swimmers. Mimi is the butterfly champion of New England in her age group, and Libby is the free-style champion of the Northeast. They have lots of medals. Libby promised to show me something about swimming because she knew I didn't get to swim much.

When we got off the bus, we were at the ocean, but there's a bay, too, that comes in at the other side of the island.

"Bay side, or ocean?" Mimi said.

"Bay now, ocean after lunch," Libby decided.

I felt good about that. Looking at the waves, I thought I'd rather be at the bay. But I was glad that Libby said it first.

We walked over to the bay. The sidewalk and sand were burning hot. The beach was so crammed that we had to step over people lying everywhere. Finally we found a spot, dropped our blanket, and jumped onto it. Our feet were burning. The breeze coming up from the water felt good after that hot bus. We stripped down to our bathing suits. "Last one in's a rotten egg—a rotten *chicken* egg!" Mimi shouted.

We practically flew down to the water, laughing and kicking sand everywhere. I could hear people shouting at us.

At the edge of the water, I shoved Mimi with my elbow, so I was the first one in.

The water felt really good. At first it was cold, but after a minute, it just felt good. There was a long rope, with floats on it. Out past the end of the rope was a raft, floating on some barrels.

We held onto the rope and went way out. Libby showed me how to do the dead man's float, lying with my face in the water and with my arms and legs just hanging there. At first I was scared, but then I did it a few times, and it felt good, floating like that.

When we swam back to the rope, Libby said I wasn't kicking like I should, and she showed me the right way to do it. After I practiced a while, it really worked. I didn't get so tired doing it her way. Libby said as soon as I learned to breathe right, I'd be a great swimmer.

After a while, Mimi said to Libby, "Race you to the float."

"I could beat you easy," Libby said.

Mimi looked at me. "It's only a little ways." She pointed to the raft. "We'll meet you there. You can swim *that* far, can't you?"

I looked at the float. It looked awfully far away.

Libby was looking at me. "Can you? Swim that far?"

I tested around for bottom with my toe. I hoped Mimi and Libby didn't notice. I could just reach bottom. "Sure," I said. I knew if I needed to, I could stand on tiptoe and still keep my head out of water.

"Really sure?" Libby sounded worried.

"'Course she's sure," Mimi said. "Libby, you act like you're the only one who knows anything about swimming. Come on!"

They were both looking at me. With their hair plastered back from their faces like that, I could hardly tell who was who, except for their voices. Libby has a regular voice, but Mimi's voice is really deep. Right then, I wished they were both Libby.

"Coming?" Mimi said, nagging. "Or are you chicken?"

"I'm coming!" I said. I was really getting mad at Mimi again.

"Okay," Mimi said. She and Libby turned around to face the float. "On your mark—get set—go!" Mimi ordered. They both took off.

I began to swim, doing it the way Libby had showed me. I didn't go very fast, but I wasn't sinking, either.

After just a few minutes, I was out of breath. I tested around for bottom. I could still stand, and I rested for a minute. Up ahead, I could see Mimi and Libby racing for the float.

I began to swim again. It was really fun. I had never swum this far before. I was getting pretty close to the float, but I knew I'd have to stop again. I was really out of breath.

I put my feet down for bottom again. I touched with my left foot, then my right and started to walk. That was fun, too. The water seemed to hold me up, and I bounced from one foot to the other. Down on right foot—bounce a little. Down on left—bounce a little. Right, left.

I was almost at the float when I came down on my right foot. There was no ground underneath me! I reached down with my toe. I went down some more. The water was beginning to cover my face. The bottom still wasn't there! All of a sudden, I was completely underwater. My whole face was covered. Where was the bottom? I began kicking really hard, the way Libby had shown me. My chest began to hurt, and my heart was pounding in my throat.

I kicked harder and used my arms, too. Suddenly, I came up above water again. Some kids on the float were watching me. I couldn't see Mimi or Libby. I called for them, but my mouth filled up with water.

I tried again to swim, but for some reason I went under again. I reached for bottom, but it still wasn't there. My whole head was under again. My heart was racing, and my throat and chest were hurting, like they were going to come apart. I tried to kick like Libby said. I kicked really hard.

I burst out on top of the water again. Two strange kids were next to me now. They reached for me, one on each side. I needed to hold on to them, to get a breath. I grabbed one of them by the neck and the other by the head. I must have held too tight because they both let go of me. I could feel them swim away.

I began to go down again. I could hear kids screaming, and then I was completely underwater. I went very far down. Finally, I could touch bottom. It was soft and squishy. I stood on my tiptoes, but I couldn't get my head out of the water. I tried jumping, but it didn't do any good.

After a minute, I didn't care. I was just tired. My chest hurt. It seemed as if it would break. I just wanted to go to sleep. I thought I was probably drowning, but it didn't matter. Only one thing mattered—I wanted to go to sleep.

All of a sudden something yanked at my hair. It pulled so hard, my hair almost came off. Someone was pulling me by the hair, pulling me somewhere, and they wouldn't stop!

They pulled harder. I wanted to cry, but I started to choke. My head hurt so! I tried to push them away, but I couldn't reach, and they wouldn't let go.

At first I didn't realize I could breathe again. I was coughing and spitting, but my face was out of the water. I began to cry.

I was standing up. I was still in the water, but I could stand! Mimi was next to me, her eyes wide. She was holding me by the hair.

"That hurt!" I said. I knew she had just saved me,

pulled me out, but it was all I could say. "That *hurt!*"
I said again, crying.

I slapped her hand away.

7

Coming home on the bus, Mimi and Libby and I were really scared—scared about what had happened, and more scared about what would happen if anybody knew about it. We promised each other we'd never talk about it, not to anybody.

I felt really bad. Dumb. I knew why I had almost drowned—just because I didn't want to be called "chicken." I think I'm probably the stupidest person in the whole world.

Mimi felt awful, too. Neither of us said anything about it, but Mimi sat really close to me on the bus. When I couldn't stop shivering, she made me use her beach towel. She has this really big one, and mine was only a regular towel from the bathroom. She said she wasn't cold, and she wouldn't take her towel back, even though she was shivering, too, and her lips were all blue.

When we got off the bus, we promised again never to tell anybody.

For the next couple days, I worked a lot helping Grandma. She was doing all the things she calls her fall housecleaning. We took down curtains and washed windows and put new curtains back up. The new curtains made everything look so different—like Grandma's house usually looks when we visit at Christmastime.

One day, Grandma asked me to bring in Ebenezer's cage off the fire escape. Ebenezer is Grandma's parakeet. She keeps him out on the fire escape in the summer, but now she was moving him back indoors for the winter.

I could hardly believe we were getting ready for winter! Every time I thought about that, about school and all, I could feel the butterflies in my stomach again. Grandma had already gone to school and signed me up, and just thinking about that made my stomach hurt.

I went down to help Grandpa in the store. He wouldn't let me mix paint, but he showed me where to find sandpaper and nails and the other things that people asked for. Sometimes, when we were alone, I could feel Grandpa watching me, as if he wanted to say something. But he never did.

There weren't any customers right then, so Grandpa and I went out and sat on the step. We looked at the street. It was awfully quiet for the middle of the day. Only a bus was at the curb, rumbling like it wished the driver would let it go.

After a minute, Grandpa spoke. "You've been awfully quiet lately." He didn't turn to look at me.

"Yeah?" I said. I pretended to be surprised. "I didn't mean to be."

Grandpa didn't answer. He just puffed at his pipe for a while. "Having trouble?" he said finally.

"Trouble? No trouble," I said. I waited for a minute. "I'm okay. I mean, it's okay about Mom and Daddy not coming back yet. I was mad at first, but it's okay now."

Grandpa nodded. "That's not what I meant."

"What then?"

Grandpa didn't say anything more.

I dug in the pocket of my jeans and found a piece of gum. I offered half to Grandpa. He took it, but he didn't chew it right away. He looked at his watch. I got really nervous. Grandpa took this little metal thing out of his pocket and began cleaning his pipe, poking and stirring around with it.

"I don't mind going to school here," I said at last. "Now that I have friends. I really like Mimi and Libby."

"Nice girls," Grandpa agreed.

I felt good when he said that. "I never had friends like them," I said.

"You have fun with them?" Grandpa said.

"Yeah. We do all sorts of stuff."

"Yes? Like what?"

I looked at Grandpa. He was holding the pipe cleaner in one hand and his pipe in the other, and he was looking at me.

I took a deep breath and turned my back, just a little. "Like going down in the sewer," I said, sort of over my shoulder.

"Fun?" Grandpa said.

"Yeah. But scary, too." I was surprised he wasn't shocked. "There's rats down there."

"I know."

"How do *you* know?" I turned and looked at him.

"Did it myself when I was a boy."

"You did? Really?"

"Yup," Grandpa said. " 'Course, they weren't sewers like we have today. They were culverts, really. Big pipes that ran underground, and we crawled through them and out under the street."

"That's what we did!" I said.

Grandpa smiled and nodded.

We were quiet for a while.

"I almost drowned!" I didn't mean to say it. I had promised not to. But it just came out.

"In the sewer?" Grandpa said, frowning.

"No! At the beach!" Then, for the first time since it happened, I started to cry.

Grandpa didn't say anything. He just sat there next to me while I cried. He nodded a couple of times and put his hand on my shoulder.

I didn't know why, but I couldn't stop crying. I couldn't even talk, I was crying so hard.

After a minute, Grandpa said, very quietly, "Just try to tell me all about it."

"I'm so . . ." I said. "It's just—everything! I'm stupid! I'm really stupid! You know what?" I was glad I was finally going to say it. "You know why I almost drowned? Because I'm stupid! Mimi wrote in her notebook that I was chicken. And so I tried to show her I wasn't! Isn't that dumb?"

Grandpa shook his head, but he didn't say anything.

"Well, isn't it? Isn't that the dumbest, stupidest thing you ever heard of?"

"I don't think that's what's important," Grandpa said. "I think what's important is that you're not ever going to do that again—are you?"

"Of course not!" I said. "Do you think I'm dumb?"

I looked at him. We both started to laugh. That made me feel better. I wiped my face on the bottom of my shirt. Grandpa handed me his handkerchief.

"What else, Jeremy?" Grandpa asked after a moment. "Anything else on your mind?"

I thought for a minute. I knew what else. And it felt good to talk. No one ever wanted to talk about that—the epilepsy. But I didn't know if I *could* talk to him. I'd never talked to Grandma or Grandpa about it before. I didn't even know what Grandpa thought about it. "It's—it's this *really* dumb thing—that's wrong with me," I said finally. I said it so softly, I could hardly hear myself.

"Do you want to tell me about that, Jeremy?"

"I don't know what to say about it. It's just—disgusting. Everybody acts like I'm sick. Crazy or something!"

"Who's everybody?" Grandpa said.

"Just everybody. All the kids. At school."

"And you're afraid of that?" Grandpa said. "Going to school again?"

"Yeah."

"Look, Jeremy," Grandpa said. "You've been here,

how long? All summer. Two months?" He waved his pipe.

I nodded.

"You haven't been sick all summer," Grandpa said. "Your mom told me before she left that you were on new medicine. Seems to me it's working pretty well." He stopped for a minute and took a breath. He hardly ever says so much at one time.

"I know," I said. I had thought about that, too. "But I didn't have any problems last summer, either. It always starts when school starts."

"It does?" Grandpa frowned.

I thought he looked worried, and that made me scared. I didn't want him to look worried. I wondered if I should tell him something. I thought I knew why the new medicine was working so well. I figured it was because of the way I'd been taking it. When I was at home, I used to take my pills one at a time. I have to take three, and I'd swallow each one by itself. But since I've been at Grandma's, I'm always in a hurry to go out after supper, so I've been swallowing all the pills at once. I put them all in my mouth at the same time and swallow them all together. I thought maybe that was what was making them work so well.

"What are you thinking?" Grandpa said.

"Something. I don't know. I was thinking about the pills. See, I swallow all three pills at once now." I said it real fast because it seemed kind of silly, saying this out loud. "I swallow them all together instead of one at a time."

I looked at him. I hoped he'd think that was what was making the pills work.

Grandpa reached over to me. He patted my shoulder. "The medicine's working, Jeremy," he said. "It's working. We don't need any magic ways to take it. It's working all by itself."

"But what if it doesn't?" I said. I began to cry.

Grandpa pulled me close and patted me a few times. I couldn't stop crying again. "The real magic," he said. "Jeremy, you already have it."

I looked at him.

He nodded. "Inside you." He smiled at me. "You'll cope just fine. Don't worry so."

8

My talk with Grandpa didn't exactly make everything better right away, but after a while I began to feel a *little* better.

When the first day of school finally came, I was excited. And nervous. I got up really early and put on my new dress. I whirled around in front of the mirror a few times, to see the skirt spin out. It's really pretty— light blue, my favorite color. The top is white, and the sleeves are really puffy, with lace all around the edges. I felt pretty in it.

I sat down for breakfast, but I was so nervous, I couldn't really eat. I was still sitting at the table when Mimi and Libby came to the door. It was only eight o'clock, and I knew school didn't start till nine.

"Jeremy! What are you doing?" Mimi said when she saw me sitting there. "Hurry up!"

"Why?" I said. But I jumped up.

"Just hurry up!" Libby added.

"Okay! Okay! I'm hurrying." I went to the mirror over the sink and began brushing my hair. I looked at Mimi and Libby over my shoulder in the mirror. They looked really nice, too. Their hair was brushed down to the side and pinned there with barrettes. I'd never seen them dressed alike before. But today they were both wearing red-checked jumpers with blue flowers on the pockets and blue blouses.

"I like your dresses," I said. "You look pretty."

"Thanks," Libby said.

Mimi made a face. "Our mother!" she said, as if that explained something.

"Your mother what?"

Libby shrugged. "Our mother says she and *her* twin always dressed alike on the first day of school!"

"BOR-ING!" Mimi said.

"I think it'd be fun," I said. I finished brushing my hair and went into the front room to say good-bye to Grandma. She was standing right by the door, cleaning Ebenezer's cage.

"Jeremy!" she said when she saw me. "Brush your hair!"

"I just brushed it!"

Grandma sighed. She pulled at my skirt and straightened my sleeves a little. Then she said something she'd said about a thousand times that morning. "Are you *sure* you don't want me to walk to school with you this morning—just this once?"

I heard Mimi in the kitchen make a sound like she was about to choke.

"I'm sure, Grandma," I said for about the thousandth time. I hugged her, really hard. "I'll tell you all about it this afternoon. Okay?"

Grandma smiled. I thought she looked a little better.

Mimi and Libby and I ran downstairs. We stopped in the store to say good-bye to Grandpa. He looked up from the counter and smiled when we came in. He just stood there for a minute, smiling and nodding.

"Lovely," he said at last.

Mimi and Libby both said, "Thank you."

I went over to kiss him good-bye. He pulled me close, and then he did something he's never done before. He kissed my cheek. "Shaky?" he asked, so quietly I knew Mimi and Libby couldn't hear.

"Little," I said. "Not too much."

Grandpa smiled. "Take care now."

"I will," I promised.

Mimi, Libby, and I went out of the store. The minute we were on the sidewalk, we started to run. We ran the whole way to school. When we got to the corner by the school, we stopped. There's a big square there, sort of a concrete platform, with some green wooden benches on it. We picked out a bench and sat down. Mimi handed me the notebook. She said all the kids had to walk by here to get to school. She and Libby would point them out to me, and I would check the notebook.

I opened the book. Robert Roda was the first to come. Libby waved to him. He didn't wave back. In the notebook, it said he was handsome. I thought he was stuck-up.

A bunch of other kids came along. There was Bruce Mueller, The Brain, also known as Lard. There was Michael Robertson, who Mimi loved. And Jay Carson with the basketball head who smelled rancid. I laughed when I saw him. His head really was round! But from our seats we couldn't tell if he smelled or not.

There was Jay Clutter, Baby Clutter—The Brat, who had to be on the same team with Jay Carson or else he wouldn't play. And Mark Vincent. Mark had a whole list: Show-off, Know-It-All, Tell-Tale, and Sneak.

And there was Andrew Malin, Weirdo. Andrew did look weird. He was wearing baggy pants and the baseball cap that Mimi told me about. He was walking funny, too, sort of bent over and looking at his feet.

Libby leaned over and whispered to me because by then Andrew was really close, "One day at school, he fainted. And he wet his pants!"

I made a face at her like I didn't believe her.

"It's true," she whispered. "Ask anybody."

I looked at Andrew close. I felt sorry for him. Then for some reason, I got really mad. He looked disgusting! Why did he have to look like that?

Mimi and Libby were poking me. Some other kids were coming.

There was Iris Kohler, Super Brain, smarter even than Bruce Mueller. There was Pat Hanratty, who could imitate anybody, especially the teachers. And Julia, with the TEETH. Julia smiled at us when she went by, but she tried to keep her mouth closed. Mimi and Libby pretended to be really happy to see her, and they said, "Hi!" in a really friendly voice. That made Julia smile, and you could see all her teeth and even her gums. She looked like a horse!

Carrie was one of the last kids to come. She looked

even littler than last time we had seen her. She was wearing this pink dress with bows. It made her look just like a baby shrimp! Mimi said her mother probably bought the dress in a baby's store. We pretended we didn't see her, and she pretended the same. But when she got real close, she waved her hand to me, a dumb little wiggle of her fingers. "Hi, Jeremy!" she said. She didn't say anything to Mimi or Libby. I didn't answer her.

We got up when two more kids came along. Mimi and Libby said they were the best kids in the class. They introduced me to Joy Shannon and Jennifer Hughes. I remembered the notebook: "Joy—Rich Kid —Spoiled Brat; Jennifer—Miss Perfect and *knows* it." But they seemed like nice kids. I wondered if they knew about the notebook.

The four of us walked to school together. I felt scared when we went in. The school was huge! But there weren't many kids around. Libby said that was because so many kids moved away. She said there were only fifteen kids in our whole class. We had twice that many in my other school! For a minute, I felt bad again, thinking about that school. I missed some of the kids and wished I were there now.

Our room was at the end of a long, ugly hall. The bottom part of the walls was painted brown, and the top sort of tan. The ceiling was so high, I could hardly see it, and the lights were hidden behind little wire cages. Everything was really dark, but you could tell it was clean because it was shiny and smelled like wax or something. There was a sign on the door of our classroom: "Fifth Grade—Miss Gladstone."

"Hoo—ray!" Mimi said when she saw it. She poked Libby. "New teacher!"

We all went into the classroom. It was bright—so different from the hall! The walls were yellow, and there were lots of windows and plants. Some of the boys were hanging out the windows, calling down to somebody on the street. All except Andrew. I noticed him right away. He was looking out a window, too, but he was sitting all by himself in the back row.

There was a piano in one corner, and the kids' desks were movable, not nailed to the floor like in my other school.

Right away, Mimi started moving the desks around, fixing them so the three of us could sit together. Joy and Jennifer lined their desks up behind ours. We were right in the middle of that when the door opened. All of a sudden, the room got really quiet.

A woman had come into the room. All the kids stood up. She was small and had gray hair, swept up on the top of her head in little curls. She went up and down the aisles, speaking to each person and shaking hands. She spoke so softly, I couldn't hear what she was saying, but the kids acted really quiet, polite, like maybe they were scared.

"Who's that?" I whispered to Mimi. "Miss Gladstone?"

Mimi didn't turn to look at me. She stared straight ahead, but she whispered, "Miss Tuller! Shhhh!"

"What's she doing here?" I whispered back. I knew Miss Tuller was the principal, but I didn't know why she was in the classroom.

Mimi didn't answer me.

When Miss Tuller got to Mimi and Libby's desks, she stopped. "Good morning, Elizabeth," she said to Libby. "Good Morning, Marion," she said to Mimi.

I stared at them. Marion? Elizabeth?

"Good morning, Miss Tuller," they both said.

"Good morning, Carrie," Miss Tuller said to Carrie, who had suddenly appeared in the aisle.

I looked at Carrie and laughed out loud! I didn't mean to. I put a hand over my mouth and pretended I was coughing.

She was standing there, pulling the sides of her skirt way out. She bent her knees and sort of dipped down, as though she were making a curtsy or something! "Good morning, Miss Tuller!" she said in this really loud, singsong voice.

I took a peek at Mimi. She had her hand over her mouth, too.

"Miss Tuller," Carrie said, "I'd like to introduce you to my new friend, Jeremy. Jeremy Martin!"

"Why, thank you, Carrie," Miss Tuller said. She turned to me. She put out her hand. Up close, she didn't look like anyone to be afraid of. "How do you do, Jeremy," she said very softly. "Your grandmother said to expect you. We're happy to have you with us."

I nodded. I wanted to say something back to her,

but I kept thinking of what Carrie had just done! For a minute, I couldn't think what to say. Finally, I just said, "Good morning."

"Good morning, *Miss Tuller!*" Carrie interrupted. "You always say someone's name when you speak to them. It's polite."

"Thank you, Carrie," Miss Tuller said again. "I think you may be excused now." She waited until Carrie went back to her desk. "Perhaps we should have a talk some day soon?" Miss Tuller said. "Get to know one another?"

I nodded.

"Friday, then," she said. "I'll expect you Friday." She went out of the room.

The whole room burst into a madhouse. Mimi and Libby finished moving the desks, and everybody started talking again. I looked at Mimi and Libby. "Hello, Marion and Elizabeth!" I said.

Mimi laughed. She shrugged. "Our big secret! You had to find out sometime! What was she talking to you about?"

"She wants to talk with me. But I don't know why."

"Don't worry," Libby said. "She probably wants to get to know you. She likes to do that. She knows all the kids in the school."

"Yeah," Mimi said. "That's why she comes in here in the morning. She says it's to say 'good morning,' but it's really to snoop around. There!" She had finished moving the desks, and they were lined up together.

We were just sitting down when the door opened again. Our new teacher came in.

Everybody in the room stopped to watch Miss Gladstone, but they didn't get as quiet as they did for Miss Tuller.

Miss Gladstone was big, probably six feet tall. She was wearing a pink dress that looked like it was too tight for her, and shiny black shoes. The shoes looked too small, too, because her feet bulged out over the tops of them. Her hair was messy—not dirty or anything, but big curls all over the place. She was pretty, though. Her face was round, sort of like a baby's. She picked up a piece of chalk and turned around to the blackboard. She wrote her name in big, neat script, very carefully—"Miss Gladstone."

Then she turned back to us. "Class!" she said.

She squeaked! Her voice was really high, like the cartoon characters in the movies. We stared without answering.

"Class?" she said again.

She sounded like Donald Duck!

Some of the kids started to laugh. Mimi and Libby both put their heads under their desks. I could hear them gasping with laughs.

"Class!" Miss Gladstone squeaked again. "My name is Miss Gladstone, and I'm your new teacher for the year."

By now everybody was laughing.

Mimi stuck her head up and poked me in the ribs. "This is going to be *some* year!" she whispered.

I started to laugh. Then for a second, I had a thought that made me feel sad, and it was a dumb thing to feel sad about: This was going to be some year, Mimi had said—but I wouldn't be here for all of it!

9

Each day after that, school got better and better. Miss Gladstone was a really good teacher. You didn't even notice her squeaking after a while. We found out she didn't squeak all the time, either—just when she got nervous or excited or something. At first, Michael Robertson and Jay Carson made fun of her a lot. But that first day, she kept them both after school. They wouldn't tell us what happened, but Jay Clutter said she kept them in until five o'clock when Michael's mother came looking for him. I didn't believe that. You're not allowed to keep kids that long. Anyway, nobody teased her much after that. She was friendly, and she made everything seem interesting.

I think I would have really loved that school, except for two things: One I was still worrying about the dumb thing that was wrong with me—not an awful lot, but I still wondered if it was going to happen again. And the other thing, the worst thing, was Carrie! She practically stuck to me. She pretended she was my best friend, and she followed me everywhere.

At first, Mimi and Libby thought it was funny. They teased me about my new "friend" and asked me when I was going to have Carrie sleep over. But one day, Carrie did something that made us all realize we'd have to do something about her.

It was the second week of school. Miss Gladstone

said that for homework we had to write an essay about what we did on our summer vacation. That way, she said, we could find out something about one another. Miss Gladstone said she'd write one, too, and next day she'd read them aloud to the class.

The next morning, Mimi was all excited. She said she had written a really great essay, but she wouldn't tell us one word about what was in it.

After lunch that day, Miss Gladstone had this big pile of papers on her desk and began to read to us from our assignment papers. Most of the papers were dull, especially the boys'. Bruce Mueller, The Brain, had spent his whole vacation going to museums in New York. "There's so much to see in New York that nobody knows about," he wrote. "Like the art exhibit at the public library. Nobody knows there's artwork there. I learned a lot this summer."

Yuck!

And then there was Jay Carson's. He went to basketball camp. "That's what you call using your head," Mimi whispered to me.

I groaned.

The other kids did the usual stuff. Some went to camp. Joy—Rich Kid—went to Europe, but she didn't tell us any of the good stuff, just about cathedrals and museums. Iris went to Israel to visit her grandparents, but it sounded like she had spent the whole summer in synagogue.

I was practically falling asleep when Miss Gladstone's voice started to squeak. I knew she was going to say something interesting. I sat up. "We have one very interesting essay here," Miss Gladstone squeaked.

I looked at Mimi out of the corner of my eye.

"Did you know that one of your classmates toured Alaska this summer?" Miss Gladstone said.

Everybody in class turned around. You could see them looking at one another, trying to find out who it could be. I looked at Mimi. Was this hers? She was just sitting there, smiling a little.

"Yes," Miss Gladstone continued. "Mimi Royce won a contest and spent two weeks in Alaska. I'd like to read this to you. She cleared her throat and read: 'For two weeks this summer, my parents sent me to Girl Scout camp. The first day there we had a competition. The person who wrote the best essay, saying why they wanted to go, would go to Alaska with one of the camp counselors. I wrote the best essay, so I won the trip. Alaska was very exciting. It was cold but not too cold. Some people wore shorts because it was summer, but there was still ice. I went ice skating in my shorts. People there keep ice in their iceboxes instead of using refrigerators. There was lots of fish in the iceboxes. I didn't eat any. I hate fish. We toured Alaska on a big bus, a triple-decker. One day, the top deck fell off, but nobody got hurt. Yours truly, Mimi Royce. P.S. Libby didn't get to go.' "

When she finished reading, everybody started talking and laughing.

Carrie's hand shot up. "Miss Gladstone, that's not tr—!"

Miss Gladstone interrupted her. "You'll have your turn in a moment, Carrie." She turned back to Mimi. "Mimi? Maybe someday you'll tell us more about it?"

I couldn't tell from her voice whether she was serious or not, whether she believed Mimi or not.

"Maybe," Mimi said.

"Did you take any pictures?" Miss Gladstone asked.

"No," Mimi said. She shook her head. "They don't have any film there. Eskimos don't like having their pictures taken."

"Well," Miss Gladstone said. "This is certainly an unusual vacation. We should definitely put this on the bulletin board for Parents' Night! If you don't mind, I'll keep this paper." She put it on the bottom of the pile and picked up another paper to read.

I looked at Mimi. "You're nuts!" I whispered. "What's going to happen when your mother sees that?"

Mimi shrugged.

"Class," Miss Gladstone said. And now her voice got really squeaky. "Class! I've saved this one for last. This essay is most unusual. It will teach us all something. It's from Carrie. Maybe you'd like to hear it."

We knew we'd have to whether we wanted to or not.

Miss Gladstone cleared her throat again. "This essay has a title. It's called, 'Friends.'

" 'I didn't go away on vacation this summer. My mother couldn't afford it. So we stayed home. But I did something important. I found out about friends. I found out who were my friends and who weren't. I made a new friend who is now in this class. Her name is Jeremy. She is my best friend. Sometimes she is mean to me. But still I know she likes me. My friend has a secret that she doesn't tell anybody. But I know she will tell me someday. That's how it is with friends."

Miss Gladstone put the paper down. The whole class was very quiet. I held my breath. I was so embarrassed, I was almost numb. That brat!

I heard Mimi make a funny sound. I looked at her. She was choking, she was trying so hard not to laugh.

She raised her hand, and there were tears in her eyes.

"Miss Gladstone," she said. "May I please be excused?"

"Certainly, Mimi," Miss Gladstone said. She said it so gently, I knew she thought Mimi was crying, from emotion or something.

I also raised my hand. "Me, too?" I said, trying to look really sad. I was so mad, I probably did. At least Miss Gladstone seemed to think so. "Certainly, dear," she said very softly.

Mimi and I went out into the hall. Mimi bent over the water fountain and took a long drink. When she stood up, she said, "Was she serious or just plain nuts for sure?"

We both laughed.

Then Mimi said, "What's she mean about a 'secret'?"

I shook my head. My stomach was doing that jumping again. "No idea," I said. I wasn't exactly lying. I didn't really know. Carrie couldn't know about it—that dumb thing. *Nobody* knew about that.

Mimi shrugged. "Probably means something about your parents being away or something?"

"Could be," I said. Carrie *couldn't* have found out—could she?

10

One morning, about a week later, Miss Gladstone had a surprise for us. Our desks had been moved all over the classroom. They were spread out now, in pairs, facing one another. We all stood there and looked.

"Just sit anywhere," Miss Gladstone said, waving her hand at us. "We'll be changing around later, anyway."

Mimi and I grabbed two desks in the back.

"What's up, you think?" I said.

"Trouble!" Mimi said.

When everybody sat down, Miss Gladstone said, "Class, we're going to spend this morning getting to know one another more."

Mimi groaned, out loud.

"Yes, Marion," Miss Gladstone said. She always calls Mimi "Marion" when she's being serious. "It's important to know one another."

"Why?" Mimi said.

Miss Gladstone sighed. "Well, Marion, you'll see. Now, this is what we'll do. I have some of your names on slips of paper here." She jiggled a paper bag for us. "The rest of you will come up and pick out a name, and whoever's name you get, you'll sit with that person and talk. You'll tell that person all about yourself, what you like, what you don't like, anything you want to tell. When you're finished, the other person will talk. Then we'll take new partners and start over again."

I looked at Mimi. She was lying, draped over her desk, her head down like she had just died.

"Why don't we just begin with the partners we have now?" Miss Gladstone said.

"Okay!" Mimi said. She sat up. She looked better. "What do you wanna know about me?"

"Anything," I said. "But you start."

"Okay, here goes!" Mimi talked real fast. "My name is Mimi. No, Marion! That's because of Libby. She couldn't say Marion when she was a baby. So she called me Mimi. And it stuck. I'm ten going on eleven. So's Libby. I like swimming. I like diving. I hate Carrie. I like dark places. Your turn!" She took a deep breath.

"Okay!" I said. I took a deep breath. I felt dumb. "I'm Jeremy. I'm ten going on eleven. I live in Long Island. My parents are in Europe. I live with my grandma and grandpa—for now. I like this school. I like reading. I hate Carrie. I have to go to the bathroom!"

"Me, too!" Mimi said. She raised her hand. "Let's ask."

I raised my hand, too. Miss Gladstone ignored us. She acted as if she didn't see us.

"Well, guess she wants us to wet our pants," Mimi said. She put her hand down.

I put my hand down, too. I didn't really have to go. I just wanted to get out of there.

"I got an idea," Mimi said. "If—"

"Mimi! Jeremy!" It was Miss Gladstone. She had

decided to notice us. "I see you're finished. Perhaps you can come up and pick out a name?"

We both went up to the desk. Mimi shook the paper bag and put her hand in as if she were fishing for a prize. She pulled out a slip of paper.

"Miss Gladstone!" she said. She held out the paper. "There's a mistake. I have Jay Carson!"

Miss Gladstone smiled. "Why is that a mistake, Marion?"

"He's a boy!" Mimi said.

Everybody started to laugh.

"We know he's a boy, Marion," Miss Gladstone said.

Mimi just looked at her. "You mean—you mean I have to talk . . . ?" She turned around and shook her head. "Forget it." She walked over and plopped down at the desk in front of Jay.

I reached in the bag and pulled out a slip of paper: Carrie Wibler. "Of course!" I thought. "Who else?"

I went over and sat down in front of Carrie. "You first," I said. I closed my eyes—tight.

"I'm Carrie Wibler and I'm eleven years old," Carrie said.

I opened my eyes. She was eleven already? She really *was* a midget! I closed my eyes again.

"I live in Brooklyn with my mother and my brother. My parents are divorced. And I don't care. My brother is very smart. He's in sixth grade. I'm smart, too. I'm in fifth grade. My best friend is . . ."

I opened my eyes again and looked at her.

"Why are you so mean to me?" Carrie said all of a sudden.

"Me?" I said, as if I didn't know what she was talking about. "Me? Mean to you?" I pointed at her. "Ha! That's a laugh!"

"You are!" she said.

I closed my eyes again.

After a minute, Carrie said, really sulky-like, "Your turn."

I took a breath, but I kept my eyes closed. "I'm Jeremy. I'm ten going on eleven. I live on Long Island. Except I'm going to school here. The end!"

After a minute, Carrie said, real quietly, "If you're not nice to me, I'm going to tell."

I opened my eyes. "Tell?"

"Yes, tell," Carrie said.

"Oh, that's nice," I said. I couldn't imagine what she was talking about, but I wasn't the least bit worried. "That's really nice. Are you going to tell me what you're going to tell?"

"You know." She was whispering. She leaned across her desk. "You're lucky I haven't told anybody yet. But Mimi and Libby's father knows about it. I showed the pill to him, down at the drugstore. He doesn't know where I got it from. I wouldn't tell him. But I might someday."

I stared at her. What was she talking about? What pill? Did she mean the pills I take? Where did she get one from?

As if she had just read my mind, she whispered, "You dropped one, you know. In the bathroom. That night at Mimi and Libby's. I saw you trying to hide them, taking them when you thought nobody was looking. Do all the kids do that? Do they all *take drugs*—on Long Island?"

I couldn't answer at first. I was just staring at her.

"You don't believe me?" Carrie said. "You better. I told you I showed it to Mr. Royce. He said it was a very strong drug, a tranquilizer or something. And dangerous. He made me give it to him. But I know it's yours!"

I started to laugh. So that's what she thought—that I was taking drugs! "Boy!" I said. "Are you *dumb*!"

Carrie just smiled at me. "I told my mother," she whispered.

I stopped laughing. I looked at her. She was still leaning over the desk. "My mother says maybe there's something wrong with you. She says she's watched you, and she always thought you were kind of strange. Is it because you take drugs?"

I stood up.

"Jeremy?" Miss Gladstone said. "Are you finished? You may change places now."

I had to get away from Carrie! I didn't care if she told the whole world I was "taking drugs." Nobody would believe that! But all of a sudden, I was worried about something else. What if she did tell, started telling everybody, and I had to explain? What if I had to tell everybody what kind of pills I was taking—and *why?* I couldn't just lie. Mr. Royce had already seen the pills. He probably knew what they were for, too.

"I won't tell," Carrie whispered. "If you're nice to me, if you're my friend. Those twins are brats, anyway. You don't have to play with them all the time. You could play with me sometimes, too. My mother says she wouldn't mind."

"Jeremy?" Miss Gladstone said. "Don't just stand there."

I went up to the desk. I could hardly think. What was I going to do? I reached in the bag and took out a paper: Joy. That was good. I went over and sat down. I couldn't think about anything except what Carrie had just said. When it was my turn to talk, I think I must have said some dumb things because Joy asked me once if I felt okay.

When it was time for new partners, I got Andrew. I sighed and went over and sat down. I decided to talk first, to get it over with. I said the same stuff I had said to everybody else. When I was finished, Andrew said, "Why are your parents in London?" He said it very quietly, and he didn't look at me.

"Business," I said.

"Do you miss them?" Andrew said. He sounded shy, and he still didn't look at me. He looked down as if he were looking into my stomach.

"Yeah. A little."

He nodded. "Do you like this school? I mean, compared to your last?"

"Oh, yeah. This is good. Better even."

He looked up and smiled. It was the first time he had looked at me. He looked really nice when he smiled. "How come?" he said.

I shrugged. "Don't know. Teacher's okay. Kids are nice. I have friends here. That makes it okay."

He was still smiling. He looked good. His whole face sort of lit up. He was the first kid who had asked me anything, as if he was really interested. I said, "How about you?"

He bent his head down again.

"Class?" It was Miss Gladstone. "I think that will be all for today. You may find your regular desks."

I stood up. I smiled at Andrew. He smiled back.

I went back to my regular seat near Mimi. Carrie stepped in front of me. "Don't forget what I told you," she said quietly.

I gave her a shove.

"Stop it!" she screamed.

"Excuse me," I said. "I'm *so* sorry!"

"You hurt me!" she screamed. "Miss Gladstone! Jeremy pushed me!"

"I did not!" I said. "It was an accident."

"Jeremy! Carrie!" Miss Gladstone said. "Please stop it! For such good friends, you certainly don't act very nice to one another sometimes." She looked at us very seriously, as if she had just had a thought. "Come to think of it," she said, "since we have all the desks moved around anyway, this would be a good time to change places. Jeremy, Carrie, you two have been try-ing to build a friendship—why don't you just choose desks together now? And anyone else who would like to may choose a new deskmate. You all know one another so much better now." She smiled at us all.

I went to my desk and began to move my things. I looked at Mimi.

"Don't worry," she said softly. "We'll teach her a real lesson. But it will take some careful planning!"

11

That afternoon, Mimi called a meeting for Friday, after school, on the steps of her house. She invited Pat and Iris and Jennifer and Joy. Even Julia, the teeth, was invited. With Mimi and Libby and me, that meant that all the girls were there. Except, of course, Carrie.

Mimi and Libby and I had discussed it. We figured we could trust everybody because everybody was fed up with Carrie. Carrie had done something rotten to each person, at least once—like going to Miss Gladstone thé day we changed seats and telling her that Jennifer and Joy were copying each other's work and that she, Carrie, felt a "responsibility" to tell. That wasn't true, and even if it was, nobody else would have told. But Miss Gladstone had separated Jennifer and Joy after that.

Another day, Iris was absent for the Jewish holidays, and that night, because Pat wasn't home, she called Carrie and asked for the homework. Carrie wouldn't give it to her. "You have to go to school every day like everybody else," Carrie told her. And she hung up on her.

But what got everybody in the class really upset was something Miss Gladstone did. She had chosen Carrie to give the "Address to the Parents" for Parents' Night. That worried us all because who knew what Carrie might say? Suppose it was something like her

"Friends" essay—or worse? Carrie wouldn't tell anybody. She made a folder for her speech and got permission to keep it in Miss Gladstone's desk. She wouldn't let anybody else see it or read it.

When we got together that day, everybody looked really serious.

"Okay," Mimi said. "What are we going to do?"

The girls looked blank.

"What do you say about getting her—but good—on Parents' Night?"

"Oh, yeah!" everybody said at once.

"How?" I said.

"That's the problem," Mimi said. "I can't think of anything. Except maybe taking all her 'Excellent' papers off the bulletin board right before the parents come."

"It's okay," I said, "but not good enough."

Everybody started coming up with ideas, but most of them were dumb ones. And the good ideas—like putting her in the dumbwaiter and leaving her there for the rest of the year—just wouldn't work.

Finally, Iris spoke. She had just been sitting there for a long time, quietly, as if she was thinking. Iris speaks English really well, even though she was born in Israel, but she still speaks slowly, as if she has to think about each word. "In Israel," she said, softly, "we have many farms. And so sometimes we have some rats. And once . . ." She stopped. She shivered. "Once, one of the boys put a dead rat in another boy's briefcase."

Everybody began screaming.

Joy held her stomach as if she were going to throw up. "Gross!"

Mimi was staring at Iris, wide-eyed. "Really? A rat?"

Iris nodded.

"O–*kay*!" Mimi said. "Okay, that's it! We get a rat!"

"Really?" Everybody was looking at her.

"Where would you get one?" Jennifer said.

Mimi looked at me and smiled. "Don't worry. Leave that part to us."

I knew what she was thinking, and I didn't like it much. "Wait a minute," I said. "This is gross! It's disgusting! She might even faint or something. And what about the rest of us? What if they found out somehow, and we all got suspended or something?"

"They'd have to suspend practically the whole fifth grade," Mimi said.

"So, maybe they would." I looked at Iris. "What happened to that kid in Israel? Did they ever find out?"

"Oh, yes!" Iris said. "He was sent away, to a school for bad kids."

Everybody started screaming again.

"No! No! Wait!" Iris said. "It wasn't just for that. He did many bad things. He was a really bad kid."

"Forget it," I said. "No rat."

Mimi just looked at me. "Chicken!" she said, smiling.

I shrugged.

"A mouse?" Julia asked softly.

Mimi glared at her. Then, all of a sudden, Mimi

started to grin. She smiled at Julia. "You're smart! You're really smart!" She turned to the rest of us. "No rat! A mouse!"

Everybody started to complain. I think all of a sudden nobody was satisfied with a mouse.

"Listen!" Mimi said. "Will you? Listen!"

Everybody got quiet. Mimi said, "I know where to get some mice, dead ones. I see lots of them at Woodfield. Now, when they've been dead a while, they get all dried up and flat. Okay! Now. You know that folder that Carrie has—the one she has her speech in for Parents' Night?"

"Yeah." We all started to laugh. We knew what was coming.

"Okay. We put the mouse in the folder. We even glue it in. Then, on Parents' Night, she gets up on the stage, opens the folder and—Ta-da!"

Everybody was talking and laughing at once. All we had to figure out now was how to get the mouse in the folder at the last minute. Julia said she would make a substitute folder, just like the one Carrie had. Mimi said she'd be responsible for making the exchange. And Mimi wasn't finished yet. "That's not all," she said. "I'm going to get a bunch of mice. We'll put them everywhere that day—in her desk, her sneakers, her pockets, her lunch box. Parents' Night is going to be *some* day for Carrie!"

Everybody was laughing and groaning. Disgusting! Gross! Just what Carrie deserved!

12

Our plans were going well. Mimi had found three dead mice at Woodfield—not as many as we hoped for, but it would do. For a week she had been "pressing" them flat between a dictionary and an atlas in her room. Now, with only two days left before Parents' Night, we had them just about ready.

Other things were going well, too. Julia had made the "substitute" folder, and it was all ready. And everybody was being really nice to Carrie so she wouldn't suspect anything.

But the best part happened by pure luck. Miss Gladstone chose Mimi to be in charge of the "arrangements" committee for Parents' Night, and that meant that we would have plenty of chance to plant all the mice we wanted. We were free to go to the auditorium after school that day to fix up the stage and the lights and all, and Mimi had chosen Libby and me to be on the committee with her. We planned to work on the mice as soon as everybody left.

That morning, I woke up with a headache. It was really bad, and I was dizzy. Grandma said I should stay home, but I told her I was all right. I knew I couldn't miss *this* day! I was probably getting a cold. *Carrie's* cold—she'd been sniffling all week.

When I got to school, Miss Gladstone had a message

for me. "Jeremy!" She motioned me to her desk. "Miss Tuller wants to see you—the minute you get in."

All of a sudden, the butterflies started in my stomach. I'd forgotten! I was supposed to have had my talk with Miss Tuller weeks ago!

I made a face. "Am I in trouble?"

"I don't know, Jeremy," Miss Gladstone said. "But I don't think so. You'd better go now, though. And don't look so scared. She doesn't bite!"

I took a deep breath and turned around to go back to my desk. Andrew was right behind, waiting to talk to Miss Gladstone. He smiled when I went by—that funny smile that made his face change so.

"It will be okay," he said. He almost whispered it.

"Hope so," I said back.

I went to my desk to put my books down. Carrie was standing there, holding a tissue to her nose. "Id something wrong?" she said in this weird voice, all stuffed up from her cold.

"Nothing that's any of *your* business!"

"Maybe id is; maybe id isn't," Carrie breathed at me.

I looked at her. She was smiling. Oh, no! Did she do something? Is that what this was all about? Did she tell—about the pills!

"What did you do?" I demanded. "Did you tell?"

"Maybe I did; maybe I didn't," Carrie said. She patted her nose, then tucked the soggy tissue in her sleeve. "You better go now," she said.

When I got to Miss Tuller's office, the door was

part-way open. I could see Miss Tuller sitting behind her desk. "Good morning, Jeremy," she said when she saw me. "Sit down." She pointed to a chair by her desk.

I sat down on the very edge of the chair.

Miss Tuller just looked at me for a minute. "Did you forget our date?" she asked very quietly.

"Yes, Miss Tuller," I said. "I'm really sorry."

"Perhaps I should have reminded you." She waited for a minute. "Well, how are you doing here?"

"Good. Very good." I felt uncomfortable.

"Any problems? Anything I can help you with?"

"No problems. Nothing." I looked at her. She was looking like she was expecting something, so I added, "I like it here, Miss Tuller. I really do. I like the kids. And I really like Miss Gladstone."

Miss Tuller nodded. "Yes, she's a good teacher, isn't she?" She smiled. "I hear you're a good student, too."

I smiled back." Uh—yeah. I mean, well—I like school. I love to read." I laughed. "My father calls me a bookworm!"

Miss Tuller laughed, too. "I know what you mean. I was a bookworm when I was your age." Then she leaned across her desk. "You appear to be the top student in your class. Did you know that?"

"Smarter even than Bruce and Iris?" I asked.

Miss Tuller laughed again. "I see you've already figured out who's who."

Miss Tuller was still leaning across her desk. "Jeremy, I've been watching you, sort of keeping track of you. And at the same time, I've heard some things about you. But sometimes, what you see and the things you hear aren't the same at all. Do you know what I mean?"

I shook my head at her. I didn't know what she meant.

"Well," she said. "For example—suppose you hear something about a person, something not very nice. But the thing you hear just doesn't seem to fit what you already know. What would you believe—what you *know* and feel about that person or what somebody told you?"

"Well, what you *know*. Of course!"

Miss Tuller nodded. "That's what I think, too," she said. She stood up and held her hand out to me. She smiled. "Good day, Jeremy."

"Good day, Miss Tuller."

I went out into the hall. I felt sort of mixed up, but I felt good, too. I thought I knew what Miss Tuller was trying to tell me—that somebody was telling her bad things about me, but that she didn't believe them. I felt good about that, good about Miss Tuller. And I couldn't wait to get back to the classroom to see Carrie. I knew she was the one who had talked, and I couldn't wait to . . .

Suddenly the floor shook! It moved! I stopped and held onto a wall. The floor moved again.

I stood very still and held my breath. I stayed there, holding on. I looked around. Nothing else was moving. I waited a minute, until the floor stopped moving.

The floor *had* moved—I was sure of it. It was shaky,

just like that time in the sewer. Yes, that's what it was! The subway! It must run under the school, just like it did by the sewer.

I felt better in a minute and went back to the classroom. Everybody was in the middle of math. I smiled at Miss Gladstone and sat down at my desk. Miss Gladstone smiled back. Then I turned and gave a big smile to Carrie. She looked surprised.

Mimi walked down the aisle to the pencil sharpener. "Was it okay?" she whispered.

"Fine," I whispered back. "Miss Tuller's really nice, isn't she?"

Mimi made a face and shrugged.

Carrie looked even more surprised.

Miss Gladstone asked us to put away our math books and get out our science books. When I reached into my desk, the floor shook again. It just dropped down!

"Oh!" I said—out loud. I couldn't help it.

"Jeremy!" Miss Gladstone said. "Is something wrong?"

"Yes! No. The floor!" I looked around the room. Everybody was staring at me.

"Is something wrong?" Miss Gladstone asked again.

"No!" I said again.

"It couldn't be," I thought. "Please no, not the epilepsy."

Miss Gladstone looked annoyed. "Please try to be quiet then."

"Yes. Okay." I bent over. I pretended I was looking

for something on the floor. This was weird! Could it only be the subway? I felt really scared. And my headache was so bad again!

At last the floor stopped moving, and I felt better the rest of the morning.

On the way to the lavatory to get washed for lunch, I asked as casually as I could, "Mimi, does the subway run under the school?"

Mimi thought for a minute. She frowned. "I don't know. It could, I suppose. Why?"

"No reason," I said. "Just wondered."

"Why?" Mimi said. "How come? Do you have an idea? Hey, that would be neat if—"

"Mi-mi!" I said. "Cut it out! I don't have any 'ideas.' It was just that I thought I felt the floor shake this morning, that's all."

"Yeah?" Mimi said. "I never noticed." She grinned at me. "I have the mice!" she whispered. "They're in a paper bag. It looks just like my lunch bag! They're all ready for this afternoon!"

"I can't wait!" I said.

"But did you know we have a problem?" Mimi said.

"Oh, no! What?"

"While you were out this morning," Mimi said, "Carrie asked Miss Gladstone if she could stay later this afternoon to practice her talk. So we're gonna have her around. But at least we'll get a chance to hear her talk."

"Nuts!" I said.

"No sweat," Mimi said. "One of us keeps her busy while the others do the stuff. We can take care of her easy."

"I guess," I said.

We went back to the classroom. The rest of the day dragged. My headache was still really bad, and I couldn't wait to get out of the classroom. I had a weird feeling, too—sort of scared, but I didn't know about what. Maybe I was scared about the mice and all—about getting in trouble.

It was right before three o'clock when it happened again. The floor fell again. It just dropped! It fell as if it had gone right out from under me. I almost screamed. But I took a deep breath and caught it. I bit my lip and held on tight to the desk. I just sat there, holding on tight.

I looked up carefully. I sat still for a long time and looked around. Everybody was getting their sweaters and lunch boxes and books. I could hear what people were saying, but they sounded so far away. The bell rang, and I heard Miss Gladstone excuse everybody. All the kids left. Miss Gladstone spoke to Mimi and Libby and Carrie and me. She said something about going to the auditorium and setting things up. I got up carefully.

"Jeremy?" Mimi said to me when we were out in the hall. "You okay?" She took my arm. She was looking at me like she was worried.

"Yeah," I said.

"You sure?" Libby said. "You don't look okay. You look funny."

"I feel funny," I said.

"What's the matter? You sick?" Mimi said. "You want to go home?"

"No." I shook my head. That made the hall move. "Let's just go to the auditorium. I'll sit down for a minute."

Libby took one of my arms, and Mimi held the other. I could hardly see where I was going.

"Is Carrie here?" I said.

"No," Mimi said. She sounded scared. "She's already in the auditorium. Are you *sure* you're okay?"

"Yeah," I said. I began to feel a little better. I could see pretty well again. We went into the auditorium.

Then, all of a sudden, the floor dropped. The walls fell in, too. I could see them coming. They fell in from the top. All of them. They came toward me. I put my hands over my head. I think I screamed.

13

When I opened my eyes, I was lying on the floor. The pain in my head moved away, just a little. And when it did, it left room for all the scared feelings. Where was I? What had happened?

I looked up. I saw feet, then faces. There was Libby and Carrie and Miss Tuller. What were they doing here? I looked around. I was in the auditorium at school. The walls and floor looked all right. They hadn't fallen down. I had!

Then I remembered. It had happened! The thing that couldn't happen here—the epilepsy! Oh, no! I closed my eyes and began to cry.

"Don't cry, Jeremy." It was Mimi. "You're okay."

I looked for her. I could hear her but I couldn't see her.

"I'm here," she said. "Back here." She put her hand on my forehead.

I looked back. Mimi was sitting on the floor behind me. I had my head in her lap. She bent over and put her face down so I could see her.

"You okay?" she said. "You really fell down hard. It's a good thing Libby and I caught you."

I couldn't say anything. I just nodded. I closed my eyes. I wanted to die, to disappear.

"Jeremy," Miss Tuller said very softly, "have you been ill lately?"

I shook my head.

"No?" Miss Tuller said. "You haven't been ill?"

"No," I said, but not very loud because my head hurt so. "I used to be sick lots," I added. "But not any more."

"What's wrong with you, Jeremy?" Miss Tuller asked, still quietly. "Do you know?"

I nodded. I opened my eyes and looked at them all. Libby and Carrie looked terrified. Miss Tuller looked serious. I looked at Mimi, but I couldn't tell what she was thinking. I knew there wasn't any sense trying to hide it any more. They'd already seen. I closed my eyes and tried to say it.

"It's—epilepsy," I whispered.

I heard somebody suck in her breath. Nobody said anything for a minute.

"How do you care for your epilepsy?" Miss Tuller asked. "Do you take medicine?"

I nodded.

"Every day? Did you take it today? Yesterday?"

"I don't know," I said. I couldn't remember! I couldn't remember anything! Why couldn't they leave me alone? I couldn't even remember why I was here. Why I was in the auditorium. I started to cry again.

"Epilepsy . . ." Libby said. It was the first time she had spoken. "Remember Gruffy, Mimi? Grandma's dog? He had epilepsy."

"Sure, I remember," Mimi said. "He died."

"He didn't die of epilepsy, dummy," Libby said. "He got hit by a car."

"I know!" Mimi said impatiently. "All I said was, 'He died.'"

"Well, you made it sound like he died of epilepsy," Libby said. "You don't die of epilepsy. The vet told us."

"I know, I know," Mimi said. "He said it was something about your brain. How the electric waves in your brain don't work right all the time when you have epilepsy. That they blow out like a storm, like a thunder and lightning storm." Mimi bent over me. "That's why Gruffy's legs got all stiff and jumpy sometimes. Like yours just did. When he had the epilepsy."

I wanted to die again, to disappear. Why didn't she stop saying that disgusting word?

"Jeremy," Mimi said, "my legs are falling asleep. Can you move your head?"

"Okay." Mimi helped me to sit up, but I couldn't get up off the floor yet. My head hurt so!

"Jeremy," Miss Tuller said, "I think I'll call your grandma."

"No. Please don't!" I begged her.

"Don't? Why not?"

"Because. She'll be so embarrassed. It's awful when I do this!"

Miss Tuller looked surprised.

"Yeah," Mimi said. "My grandma thought it was awful, too. She wanted to get rid of Gruffy."

"Well, *I'm* not Gruffy!" I said to her. I was mad all of a sudden. "I'm a person. Not a dog!"

Mimi looked surprised. She stood up. "I know you're not a dog!" she said. "I never said you were!"

I stared at her hard. "You don't know what it's like! Nobody knows what it's like!"

"What *is* it like, Jeremy?" Miss Tuller asked very quietly.

I looked at her. I looked at them all. They were so quiet . . . watching me.

"It's like—well, like you said—a storm. It's like everything starts moving, inside you and out. But you don't feel—I mean, it doesn't hurt or anything. You don't even know what's happening. But you sort of faint. And when you wake up, everybody acts stupid. Like you've done something awful."

"I didn't think it was awful," Mimi said. "You just looked weird." She came over to me and put her face close to mine. "You okay now?" she whispered.

I nodded.

"Libby and I didn't know what to do," Mimi said, "when the epilepsy started. So we didn't do anything."

I could feel the tears coming up again.

"You're not supposed to do anything," I said. "Just . . . keep me from hurting myself when I fall down. Or . . ." I could barely bring myself to say the rest. I said it really quietly. "Or be sure I don't hurt myself if I—roll around."

Mimi nodded.

"I still think we should call your grandma," Miss Tuller said. "She has to know, anyway."

"I know," I said. "But I'll tell her later, after I get home. I don't want her to come and get me. I hate that!"

Miss Tuller nodded understandingly.

"I don't think you should let her do that, Miss Tuller." It was Carrie. We all stared. It was the first time she had said anything. I had almost forgotten she was there!

"I don't think you should let her do that," Carrie said again. "I don't think she should go home by herself! I think you should call her grandmother and she should come and get her. I think Jeremy should be watched. My mother says people with epilepsy are retarded!"

"She's crazy," said Mimi.

But Carrie pretended she didn't hear her. She came closer to me. I could see Mimi's ring with the seagull on her finger. "*I* think," she said, "that when people have a disease like that, they should *tell* other people! *I* think you should tell everybody in school so they'll know what's *wrong* with you."

"*I* think *you* should shut up!" Miss Tuller said.

Carrie gasped.

We all stared at Miss Tuller. She looked very calm, as if she hadn't said anything. She came over to me and reached out her hand. At the same time, Mimi reached down to help me, too. They collided, and Mimi lost her balance. She fell against Carrie, and Carrie fell down on the floor, hard. Her papers and books flew all over.

"Stop it!" she screamed. "You did that on purpose!"

Nobody even looked at her. She scrambled around on the floor, trying to get her papers together.

Miss Tuller helped me to my feet, and we walked to her office.

Miss Tuller made a deal with me. She said she wouldn't call Grandma if I would go home in a taxi. I thought that was dumb because Grandma's house is only three blocks away, but Miss Tuller wouldn't let me walk there. She sent Mimi and Libby with me in the cab and paid the driver herself when he came.

When we got to the corner by the store, I got out. I didn't want Grandma and Grandpa to see me in the taxi and start asking questions right away. I just wanted a chance to think for a minute. I said good-bye to Mimi and Libby.

Libby squeezed my hand. "See you tomorrow," she said.

Grandma and Grandpa were in the store, and I shouted, "Hi! I'm home!" and ran upstairs. I did that because I run upstairs every day. But it really made my head hurt. I hoped Grandma wouldn't come up to see me.

When I got to my room, I lay down on the bed. I thought my head would break. Even the pillow made it hurt. I lay there, trying to think, to remember what had happened, but I must have fallen asleep.

When I woke up, it was dark and Grandma was shaking me lightly. "Jeremy! Wake up. Suppertime. And Mimi's on the phone."

I sat up. For a minute, I didn't know where I was or what was happening.

"Telephone," Grandma said again. "You must have

been awfully tired. You fell asleep right after school."

"Oh, wow!" I rubbed my face. I felt a little better. "I'm coming."

I went out to the kitchen. It was so light, it hurt my eyes. It felt weird waking up like that and finding it was dinnertime.

I picked up the phone. "Jeremy!" Mimi said. "You okay?"

"I think so," I said. "I just woke up."

There was a pause for a minute. Then Mimi said, "Libby and I did some work on the notebook this afternoon. On your page." She paused again.

I held my breath. The notebook! What had they written—now that they knew? "Yeah?" I said finally.

"Yeah. We took out a word. You know the one— 'chicken.' "

I laughed. "O-*kay*!" I said. "Okay!"

Mimi laughed, too. "Okay," she said. "See you."

"See you," I said. I hung up and sat down at the table.

Grandma and Grandpa were waiting for me. I ate dinner pretty well. When it was almost over, I told them what I knew I had to say. "Uh—something happened at school today."

"Yes?" Grandma said. "What?"

"I got sick."

"What?" Grandma said. "Sick? What do you mean, sick?"

"Sick, like—you know." I didn't know how to say it. They were both staring at me. Grandpa had been lighting his pipe, and he held it in one hand and the match in the other, just looking at me.

"Do you have a cold?" Grandma asked.

"*No*, I don't have a *cold*." I knew I'd have to get this over with. "I had one of those—you know—the *epilepsy*."

Grandma just stared at me. I didn't want to look at Grandpa.

"No! Oh, no!" Grandma said at last. "Are you all right?" She came around the table and put her hand on my forehead, as if she were feeling for a fever or something. "Are you all right now?"

"Fine. I'm really okay."

"You sure?" Grandma said. "Why did that happen?" I shrugged.

"Should I call the doctor?" Grandma was looking at Grandpa.

"No!" I said. "Don't! I'm really okay. This used to happen lots of times, and Mom never had to call the doctor. Only the first time, or when I had my medicine changed or something."

"Your medicine!" Grandma said. "Your medicine! Have you been taking it?"

"Yes." I nodded. But I knew that wasn't exactly true. Lately, I'd been taking my medicine at night when I went to bed, instead of at dinner. And twice last week, I was already in bed when I remembered. I didn't want to get up to get a drink, so I promised myself I'd take it next morning. But now I couldn't remember whether I had or not.

Grandma went to the shelf where I keep the pills. She came back with the bottle and poured out three pills. "Take these," she said. "Right now. And I want to *see* you take them from now on."

She went over to the sink to get me a drink of water.

"How did it happen?" Grandpa asked very softly.

I shrugged. "Nothing much. I just felt funny all day. And then after school, in the auditorium, it happened."

"*After* school," Grandpa said. "That's good. Who was with you?"

"Mimi, Libby, Carrie, Miss Tuller." I listed the names on my fingers.

"And then?" Grandpa said.

I knew what he meant. He wanted to know how everybody acted, if it was okay. I wasn't sure if I could talk about it. I didn't really know yet. Miss Tuller acted okay. Mimi and Libby were okay. Carrie acted like a jerk, but Carrie always does. "I don't know," I said finally. "I think it was okay, but I'm not sure yet. Mimi said I looked weird, but she said it wasn't awful."

Grandpa nodded.

Grandma was standing there with my water, and I took my pills. Then she started clearing the table, taking things over to the sink. She moved very fast, and she scrubbed and wiped everything as she went. She always acts like that when she's upset.

"Jeremy?" Grandpa said when Grandma was across the room. "Have you really been taking your medicine?"

"No," I said. "Not all the time." I didn't dare look at him. I waited, but he didn't say anything more.

I looked over at Grandma across the room. Her back was to me, and she was bending down, getting the dishpan out from under the sink. I looked at Grandpa. "I didn't mean to," I whispered. "It wasn't on purpose. I just forgot."

Grandpa nodded. "A lot?" he asked.

"No. Just twice, I think."

"On purpose?"

"No! I already told you. I just forgot. I was already in bed, and I didn't want to get up again, but I was going to take it next day."

Grandpa nodded again. He was silent for a while. "What's going to happen tomorrow?"

"Don't know."

"Worried?"

"A little. Carrie."

"She'll tell everybody tomorrow, huh?"

"Yeah. She'll make it sound awful, too."

"Mimi and Libby?" Grandpa asked. "How will they be?"

I shrugged. "Okay. I'm not sure, but I think they're okay."

Grandpa pushed his chair back from the table. His pipe had gone out, and he lit it again. I watched him holding the matchbox over the pipe bowl, lifting it up and down while he puffed until it was lit. "So," he said. "Sounds like Carrie's the only real problem."

"Yeah," I said. "She always is. And I don't know what we can do about her, either."

Grandpa took his pipe out of his mouth. He smiled at me. "I have an idea you might come up with something," he said.

14

The next morning, Mimi and Libby stopped for me much earlier than they usually do. Mimi was carrying a paper bag.

"You okay?" they both said as soon as they saw me.

"Yeah," I said. "What's that?" I pointed to the bag.

Mimi grinned. She looked around to see if Grandma was in the room. "Three *flat* mice!" she whispered.

I felt confused. "I thought we were going to do them yesterday," I said. I tried to sound real casual. I felt dumb that I couldn't remember. I always forget things that happen just before I have one of those epilepsy-seizure things.

"We couldn't," Libby said. "Remember? You got sick first?"

"Oh, yeah. I remember." But I didn't. I could hardly remember anything about yesterday after leaving the classroom.

"Let's go," Mimi said.

I said good-bye to Grandma, and Mimi and Libby and I ran the whole way to school.

When we got inside, it was dark. Nobody was there yet, not even Miss Gladstone.

"Let's go!" Mimi said.

We went into the classroom very quietly, and right to Carrie's desk. Mimi took out the pencil case and opened it. Every single pencil was in it, and they all had their points sharpened. There wasn't room for even a little mouse.

"Guess we have to get rid of some pencils," Libby said. She dumped some out of the box. Mimi took out a mouse from the bag. She stuffed it, head first, into the pencil box. Only the tail stuck up. She snapped the box closed, then put another mouse inside the cover of her loose-leaf book.

"Let's get out of here before we get caught," said Libby.

We picked up our books and things, turned out the lights, and tiptoed out of the building. We ran back toward the corner where everybody meets.

When we got there, we could see all the girls standing in a circle. Somebody was in the middle of the circle talking—Carrie! When we got closer, we could hear her. "And then!" she said. "And then she just went, 'Ooh'—and she fell down flat on the floor! *I* grabbed her! But she was drooling, and everything. So I ran and I got Miss Tuller . . . ."

Carrie stopped. She had seen Mimi and Libby and me standing there. Everybody turned to see why Carrie had stopped.

"Jeremy!" Iris said when she saw me. "What are you doing here? Carrie said you were sick! You look okay to me."

"Carrie's a liar!" Mimi said, before I could say anything.

"I am not a liar!" Carrie said. She smiled that stupid smile at me. "You are sick, aren't you, Jeremy?" She looked at the other girls again. "Jeremy has epilepsy!" she said. "She had a *fit* yesterday. Didn't you, Jeremy?"

"Liar!" Mimi said.

I didn't know what to say. Everybody was looking at us, as if they were trying to figure out who to believe.

I was scared, but I knew I had to say something. "I didn't have a '*fit*,'" I said. "But I did—I mean, I do —have epilepsy." I said it very quietly.

"Yeah," Mimi said. "And Carrie got so scared, she wet her pants!"

Everybody started to laugh. Carrie looked furious. "Let's go," Mimi said.

We started back to school. When we got to the classroom, Miss Gladstone took me out in the hall and asked me about a million times if I was *really* all right. I promised her I was. While we were talking, over her shoulder I could see Mimi grinning at me from the classroom door. She had her thumb and one finger squeezed together, and she was waving her hand round and round in a circle, pretending she was swinging a mouse by the tail. For the first time in about forever, I felt like laughing.

Finally, Miss Gladstone let me go back in the classroom. The morning began normally enough. Miss Gladstone had us start with our math books, but since we hadn't put any mice in Carrie's, nothing happened. But then Miss Gladstone handed out our math papers and had us take out our loose-leaf books.

I held my breath and got out my book. I didn't dare

look at Carrie. We had put the really big mouse inside her loose-leaf book. I kept my head down and carefully unsnapped the rings of my book.

Out of the corner of my eye, I could see Carrie pull the book out of her desk. She lifted it up and put it on the desk. As she lifted it, the mouse slipped out. It just plopped quietly onto Carrie's skirt—right in her lap! She didn't notice it. I bit my lip. I could feel Mimi looking at me. The mouse just lay there in Carrie's lap while she fixed her papers.

I peeked over. Carrie finished putting the papers in the notebook, closed it, then bent over to slide the book into her desk. That's when she saw the mouse. And that's when she started to scream. I put my hands over my ears.

Everybody turned around and stared. Miss Gladstone came running down the aisle and saw the mouse in Carrie's lap. She picked it up, walked over to the wastebasket, and dropped it in. Then she went back to Carrie's desk. "Where could it have come from?" Miss Gladstone asked. She seemed puzzled. She looked up in the air as if she thought it might have fallen out of the ceiling.

Then she looked at Carrie. Carrie wasn't screaming any more, but she was sniffling as though she were crying.

"Carrie," Miss Gladstone said, "why don't you go to the lavatory for a minute and wash up. You'll feel better." She turned to the rest of us. "And while Carrie's doing that, why don't you all just get out your drawing pencils and work on your posters for the bulletin board? We'll finish those now so everything will look nice tonight when your parents come. I'll get the paints for those who need them."

I looked at Mimi. She smiled. None of the other girls dared look at one another.

In a minute, Carrie came back and sat down. She took out her pencil box and immediately began to shout. "Miss Gladstone! Miss Gladstone! Some of my pencils are missing!"

Miss Gladstone looked annoyed.

"The box was full yesterday. Ooooh!" All of a sudden, she started to scream again. "There's a mouse in here!" She flung the box away. It went flying across the room and landed right by Mimi's desk. Pencils went spilling everywhere.

Mimi bent over and picked up the box. She peeked inside. "Miss Gladstone, there *is* a mouse in here! Maybe *it* ate the pencils." She wrinkled up her nose and peeked in the box again. "But it's dead now."

Miss Gladstone came down the aisle. She looked in the box. "It is a mouse," she said. "And it is dead." She looked around. "The rest of you—have you seen any mice anywhere?"

Everyone shook their heads.

I didn't dare look at anybody.

"I know," Mimi said. "Carrie keeps candy in her desk. Maybe that's what attracts the mice."

"I do not!" Carrie said. "Maybe you're the one who put the mice there!"

"Now, why would Mimi do that?" Miss Gladstone said. "Carrie—"

"Because she hates me!" Carrie screamed. "They all hate me! Everybody hates me!" Suddenly, she grabbed her poster off her desk and started to rip it up. "You all hate me! I'm getting out of here. And I'm not coming back!" She threw the pieces of poster all over the floor. Then she headed for the door. "You can do your old Parents' Night without me. I'm not coming back! And I'm not giving the stupid 'Address to the Parents,' either!" She ran out of the room and slammed the door.

It got very quiet in the classroom. We all stared at one another and at Miss Gladstone. Somebody giggled once, but Miss Gladstone just glared at her.

"All right, class," Miss Gladstone said after a minute. "Please just go on with your work. I'll be right back." She opened the door and went out, leaving the door open.

I peeked over at Mimi and Libby. Libby looked scared. Mimi made a face and shrugged her shoulders, but I could tell she was scared, too.

I felt funny—sort of guilty. I tried to work on my poster, but I couldn't. Carrie was a brat. She deserved everything she got. Then why did I feel guilty?

Miss Gladstone was gone a long time. We all worked very quietly. I think everybody was scared. Finally, there was a little tap on the door. I looked up. Miss Tuller was in the doorway, looking right at me. She beckoned when she saw me looking at her.

"Jeremy?" she said quietly. "Would you step into the hall for a minute?"

Oh, no! She knew! My heart was beating so hard in my throat, I could hardly swallow. I stood up slowly and went into the hall. I could feel everybody's eyes following me.

Miss Tuller led me away from the door a little. "Jeremy," she said, "I've just heard what happened. I'm—I'm quite upset. And since Carrie won't be coming back tonight . . ." She was looking at me, hard, without smiling or anything. "I'd like you to give the 'Address to the Parents.'" She paused and just looked at me. "The theme is *friendship,* you know."

I just stared at her. What did she mean? Did she know . . . ? I swallowed. "But I can't, Miss Tuller! I mean—Carrie will be back! She was just upset. She'll change her mind! She'll—"

"I don't think so," Miss Tuller interrupted. "I would like you to do this. Miss Gladstone will give you time to prepare." She was still looking at me with that look, as if she knew about what we'd done. Then why didn't she say something?

I could feel that thing in my stomach, that weird feeling I get when I'm scared. I couldn't even look at Miss Tuller. "Yes, ma'am," I said.

I knew I'd have to do it. I went back into the classroom. Miss Tuller didn't even say, "Thank you." She just walked away.

As soon as I got back to my seat, Mimi came over. She kept an eye on the door, watching for Miss Gladstone or Miss Tuller. "What happened?" she whispered. "Does she know it was us?"

"I don't know," I whispered back. "She didn't say anything. But she wants me to give the 'Address to the Parents.' She found out Carrie wasn't coming back."

"Whew!" Mimi said. She sounded relieved. She grinned at me. "Lucky! I thought for a minute we were in big trouble. Well, at least we don't have to switch the folder for her speech." She smiled again and went back to her desk.

I didn't know why she felt so relieved. I felt awful. Did Miss Tuller really know? She had been so nice to me before. Why did I feel so worried about Carrie? She was a brat!

And what was I going to say in the speech? I put away my poster and started on the speech. I worked hard on it. I wrote it and tore it up and wrote it again. I had to say something—about friendship. What? I worked on it all afternoon. Miss Gladstone finally came back to the classroom, but there was no sign of Carrie. Miss Gladstone didn't say anything about her, and nobody dared to ask.

When we were finally dismissed that day, I took the speech home with me to work on some more. I knew it was going to be important. And there were some special things I wanted to say.

15

When I got home that afternoon, there was a letter for me on the little table by the telephone in the kitchen. I recognized it right away—my mother's handwriting and the thin envelope and funny stamps. I sat down at the table to read it. It was very short. "Dear Jeremy," it said. "Everything's going really well, and so fast! Daddy's business is almost finished already. We'll be home sooner than we thought—long before Christmas! Maybe even by Thanksgiving. Now, didn't that time go fast? As soon as we have a definite date for leaving, we'll call. We can't wait to see you. We have some wonderful presents for you. Love, Mom and Daddy."

I looked up from the letter. Grandma was cutting me a little piece of cake at the table. I looked at her and held out the letter. I felt strange. "They're coming home," I said. Somehow, I didn't feel so happy. I mean, I felt sort of happy, but I felt sad, too.

Grandma took the letter from me. I watched her reading it. She looked up from it and smiled at me. "Are you pleased?" she said.

"I don't know," I said. "I mean—yes. I guess so." I got up from the table. "I have something to do. I have to work on something for tonight."

I took my cake and my books and went into the front room. I put my things down on the table by the window and looked out. I was going to miss this place! I sat down and tried to concentrate on the speech, but I could hardly think. I kept thinking about Mom and Daddy. I was glad they were coming home. I wished so much they could be here tonight for Parents' Night. But, why did I feel sad, too? I guessed I was going to miss everybody—Mimi, Libby, Grandma, Grandpa—Grandpa, especially. What was the matter with me? Why do I always feel two ways at once? It was just like this afternoon at school. Why can't I feel either happy *or* sad, like normal people do? Why do I feel both ways at once?

In a little while, Grandma called me to dinner. We were eating early so we could be ready for Parents' Night.

Grandpa looked at me when I sat down at the table. "How did it go today?" he said softly.

For a minute, I didn't know what he meant. But then I remembered. He meant about the epilepsy, and the kids.

"It was okay," I said. "It really was." I picked up my fork and started to eat. "Carrie was a pain. But Carrie's always a pain."

Grandpa smiled. "You look pretty good."

"I *feel* pretty good." I looked at him. "Did you hear about Mom and Daddy?"

He nodded. "I heard."

I just looked at him for a minute.

He looked back. "And?"

"Nothing." I shook my head. I was afraid if I said any more, I would begin to cry. This was weird! I was happy! Then why was I crying? I bent my head over my plate and finished my dinner in silence.

I looked up once when Grandma got up to clear the table. Grandpa was looking at me.

I smiled at him, but I could feel the tears coming again, too. And suddenly, I was nervous, scared about tonight.

"What is it?" Grandpa asked. "There's something else?"

I nodded. "It's tonight. I have to give the 'Address to the Parents.'"

Grandpa didn't even look surprised. He just waited for me to go on.

"It's—well, it's not just the speech. It's something about Carrie. We were mean to her today. She deserves it, but—I don't know. The theme is friendship. I don't know what to say. I've worked on it all afternoon, and I still don't know if I have the right words."

Grandpa nodded. He took his pipe out of his pocket and tapped it gently for a minute. "You know," he said finally, looking up at me, "sometimes it doesn't matter a lot how you say something. It's the meaning that counts."

I nodded. "Yeah, but that's just the problem! I don't know—"

Grandpa interrupted me. I don't think he's ever done that before. When he spoke, he sounded so serious.

"I think that whatever you mean to say tonight will come through if you're sincere, no matter what words you find to use."

I thought about that. I had the feeling that Grandpa had just said something really important.

Grandpa nodded, as if he knew what I was thinking. He reached over and patted my hand.

We both helped Grandma with the dishes and clearing up. When she heard I was giving the speech, she got all nervous, but I told her it was all right. I hoped it was!

We all got dressed up then and left for school. I put on my prettiest dress, the one Grandpa had bought me for the first day of school.

Grandpa looked very serious when we left, but he didn't say anything. I wondered if he was still thinking about what he had said before—that it's the meaning that counts.

When we got to school, there was already a bunch of people in the auditorium. I saw Mimi and Libby right away, and went to sit with them. All the kids were sitting together in the front of the room.

"How do you feel?" Libby said as soon as she saw me. "You scared?"

I nodded. "Yeah. My knees are shaking. I can hardly stand up." I meant it, too. My knees were *really* shaking.

"Boy!" Mimi said. "Maybe you'll fall off the stage!"

"Thanks," I said, but I laughed.

"Think scaredy-cat Carrie will come?" Mimi said.
I shrugged. "Don't know. What do you think?"

Mimi shrugged, too. "Don't know. Don't really care."

I looked at her. I wondered if she meant that. I wondered if she felt a little bad, too. But she didn't say anything more.

After a few minutes, the auditorium was practically full. Miss Gladstone went up on the stage. She stood there, waiting for everybody to get quiet. Then, when she had their attention, she started to talk. "Welcome to Parents' Night," she said. "Since the students organized this program, it's only fair that they run it. However, I'd like to take a minute to introduce our first speaker for the evening. I do want you to know, though, that Jeremy is a last-minute speaker. We had a quick change of plans today, so Jeremy hasn't had much time to prepare. The theme of her speech is friendship. I'm sure that what she has to say will be of interest to all of us. Parents, I'd like to introduce— Jeremy Martin!"

There was an applause, and Miss Gladstone stepped down from the stage. I went up. My knees were still shaking. I wondered for a minute if I really would fall off the stage. I walked to the lectern and held on, really tight. Then just as I began to speak, I saw Carrie! She had come in the back door with her mother, and her mother was holding her hand, as though she were a tiny little girl.

"Miss Tuller, teachers, parents," I said. "Grandparents! Welcome to Parents' Night." I looked down at all the faces. I could see Grandma and Grandpa, smiling at me.

I looked back at my paper. "I'm new in this school," I read. "At first, I didn't want to come here because I hardly knew anybody. I thought that at recess and all I'd have to be by myself when everybody else had somebody to talk to and play with. And that would feel awful. And I didn't want to come here because . . ."

I paused. I looked up from my paper. I saw Miss Tuller and Miss Gladstone, Mimi and Libby. I saw Andrew. Everybody was looking at me, as if each person was waiting for something. ". . . because I was afraid that even if I did make friends, it wouldn't last. But I found out that I could make friends pretty fast. And I found out that they'd stay friends because they don't care *too* much about—certain things. Because a friend doesn't really care . . ." I took a deep breath. "A friend doesn't *really* care if you're—different in some ways."

I looked up. All of a sudden, I was looking straight at Andrew. I hadn't planned to say it, but suddenly I was saying, "Like, a friend doesn't *really* care if you—talk or *walk* different from the way everybody else does."

I thought Andrew smiled. And just as I was getting ready to look back at my paper, I saw Carrie. She was still sitting next to her mother, not with the rest of the kids up front. Her face looked as if she'd been crying.

Then I said something else I hadn't planned to say. "And a friend can be—a friend can even be—somebody who's mean to you sometimes."

Carrie looked surprised.

I couldn't help smiling. "And so," I said. "I like this school. I like the teachers."

I saw Mimi and Libby grinning at me. I couldn't help grinning back. "And I like the kids!" Then I said the rest really fast because I was beginning to feel embarrassed. "And I hope you enjoy Parents' Night!" I hurried off the stage.

There was a big applause. I felt really good. Just as I was stepping down from the stage, I saw Grandpa. He was smiling. All that worried, serious look he had had before was gone.

In the crush of people going down the hall to the classrooms, I could see Miss Gladstone trying to get to me. I was following Mimi and Libby, who ducked into the lavatory. Suddenly, Carrie stepped in front of me. She wasn't with her mother any more. "Jeremy?" she said. She sounded funny, sort of shy. "Jeremy, that was a really nice speech."

For a second, I just stared.

"I mean it," she said. "It was really nice. Better than the one I had prepared."

"Thanks, Carrie," I said. "Hey, thanks for saying so."

She smiled at me. It looked like a real smile, too. She turned and disappeared down the hall to the classroom.

I went into the lavatory.

"Hey, Jeremy!" Mimi said. "That was a neat speech!"

"Thanks," I said.

"It was really good!" Libby added.

"What do you think Carrie thought?" Mimi said. "Did you see her hanging on to her mother?"

I didn't answer.

Mimi was looking at me. "You seem different tonight," she said. "All day, even."

"Really? I didn't mean to."

"Oh, it's okay," Mimi said. "It's not *bad*—just different. Old. Grown-up or something."

I laughed. "That's because I'm almost eleven. Next month!" That reminded me. My birthday was next month—and my parents would be home! I felt better again. I looked at Mimi and Libby. "My parents are coming home soon," I said.

"What? When?" They were both staring at me.

"Soon. A few weeks."

"But you said Christmas!" Mimi said.

"I know. But I got a letter today. They're coming back in maybe a few weeks."

Libby was looking at me like she was going to cry. "You can't!"

"We were just getting started!" Mimi said.

"I know. What can I do?"

"That's rotten." Mimi said. "Really, really rotten!" She plopped back against the wall.

"Hey, Mimi," I said. "I'm not going to die! I'm not

even leaving. At least not yet. And when I do, you two can come visit. And I'll be back next summer."

They both looked happier then—a little.

"Come on!" I grabbed their arms. "We have lots of time yet."

Mimi's eyes began to light up. "Yeah," she said. "And I almost forgot. Halloween's coming. I can think of *lots* of ways to spook Carrie!"

"Come on," I said. "Everybody's waiting." We rushed out of the lavatory and down the hall to our classroom.

Miss Tuller was waiting at the door. "Congratulations, Jeremy," she said as soon as she saw me. She didn't look angry, the way she had that afternoon. She was smiling at me. "Very well done," she said.

"Thank you," I said.

"You expressed it so well, about friendship," Miss Tuller continued. "You seemed—I mean, how did you know . . . " She paused.

"About friends? About real friends?" I asked.

She nodded.

I looked at Mimi and Libby. I smiled.

They grinned back.

"I've—had a lot of help," I said.

MS READ-a-thon—
a simple way to start youngsters reading

Boys and girls between 6 and 14 can join the MS READ-a-thon and help find a cure for Multiple Sclerosis by reading books. And they get two rewards — the enjoyment of reading, and the great feeling that comes from helping others.

Parents and educators: For complete information call your local MS chapter. Or mail the coupon below.

Kids can help, too!